How
MOM
Got A
Life!

Also By Sheelagh Mawe

Dandelion - TUT, 1994
Grown Men - Avon Books, 1997
The Most Important Lesson of All - TUT, 2003

• • • • • • •

More from www.tut.com or
at bookstores everywhere:

Dandelion
Sheelagh Mawe, 1994

The Most Important Lesson of All
Sheelagh Mawe, 2003

Totally Unique Thoughts,
Reminders of Life's Everyday Magic
Mike Dooley, 1998

Lost in Space
Mike Dooley, 1998

Thoughts Become Things * LIVE!
Audio Tape/CD, Mike Dooley, 2001

Infinite Possibilities:
The Art of Living Your Dreams
Audio Program, Mike Dooley 2002

Notes from the Universe, Books 1-3
Mike Dooley, 2003

A novel

How
MOM
Got A
Life!

SHEELAGH MAWE

TOTALLY UNIQUE THOUGHTS®

For
Amanda

Much loved daughter...
Family defender...
Best friend!

ONE

When it was all over and Mom had proved her point or, as she liked to put it, pulled off her "coup", and we were telling people what she did, old Mrs. Simmons, who lived next door and baby-sat us when we were little said, "It was faith that did it! Faith, pure and simple."

Mom's brother, Paul, our family's candidate for the Guinness Book of World Records for skepticism and whose favorite comment is, "If you believe that, you'll believe pigs fly over Times Square," said, "You should see the pigs flying over the square! Herds of them!"

And Mom, who after all did it, said, "I kept telling you, you get what you think about. Maybe now you'll believe me."

My sister, Mary, who was painting her inch-long, fake nails a sickly mauve at that particular time, said, "I thought you'd gone menopausal on us, I really did. That is," she hurried on, seeing Mom's eyes narrow, "until you did it. Then, of course, I knew right-off you'd just been thinking those good thoughts."

"I thought you were crazy," I told her. "I mean really far out, earth-to-Mom, C-R-A-Z-Y."

And I had. I mean, mothers don't go around doing what my mother did that day. Not any mothers I know about anyway.

Before I tell you what she did though, I need to tell you more about us so you'll know, like they say, where we're coming from.

I guess you could say it all started back when Mom and Dad got divorced. That's all a long time ago now, I'll be a college freshman come September, but it was in the years right after the divorce that things got really interesting and led to Mom pulling off her coup.

In those same years Dad went through so many new wives Mary said it was a wonder the phone company didn't charge him extra for listing all the ex's in the phone book. Weird how he stayed with Mom eighteen years and didn't make it eighteen months with any of the others. Going to his weddings turned into an annual event for us kids, like Christmas. And you should have seen some of the step brothers and sisters we picked up along the way! Whoa! I'm not going to get into them though because they're not important to this story and because, like Mary always said, "They're temps! You know, here today and gone tomorrow. Just like the wives. Don't let 'em get to you, kid."

I was eleven when Dad left. Mary, fifteen and Steve, my brother, sixteen.

I remember how we were all in the living room not looking at one other the Sunday when, right after lunch, Dad went and packed a suitcase, mumbled something about seeing us later, and walked out the door just as if he was going off on another business trip. What really seemed weird at the time was that we were in the living room at all because, except for Christmas and when we had company, we never used it. But anyway, maybe because it was in the front of the house and that's as far as we could go without going out and getting in the car with him, that's where we ended up, all of us sitting on the edges of chairs like we didn't belong there.

We heard his car roar up the street, heard him slam on the brakes at the STOP sign at the top, then take off again. We listened till the sound of the car's motor faded into the usual sounds of a hot, Florida Sunday afternoon: a lawn mower droning down the block a-ways, whoever pushing it in no big hurry to finish; the roar of a Boston Whaler making a fast turn out on the bayou back of our house, followed by screams and laughter so you knew whoever was skiing off the back hadn't made the turn. I remember wondering how come other people's lives seemed to be going on like normal when it felt like ours was falling apart. And I wondered, too, if Dad turned left or right up there at the STOP sign though I never have thought to ask him.

Out of the corner of my eye I could see Steve working a swirling pattern in the old shag carpet with his bare toes and Mary's fingers busy tying knots in the tassels of a cushion she'd put on her lap. My eyes blurred right about then though and everything went out of focus and just when I thought the lump in my throat was going to choke me, I heard a sound like a hiccup and looking up saw that Mom was crying and must've been for quite a while from the look of her.

"Not," she blubbered, seeing all of us staring at her, "because this divorce is a bad thing. It isn't. It's for the best. People change. Your father wants... That is... Times change. It's just," and she'd rubbed at her eyes and blown her nose, "...it's just the lost dreams, you know? The goals we set that will never be met. It's hard, painful, to give them up even though you know you've outgrown them. Do you understand what I'm saying?"

Steve and Mary mumbled, "Yeah... Kind've..." and I sort of nodded though I have a much better idea of what she meant now than I did back then.

Dad hadn't been gone half an hour than Mom started losing it over money. "We better turn the A/C off," she said, heading for the thermostat in the hall. I heard the motor cut off with a thunk and I felt like a friend had just died.

"It's ridiculous having the thing running night and day, day and night," she'd gone on, coming back into the room. "A little heat never hurt anyone. It helps to remember that people lived for thousands of years before someone got around to inventing air conditioning."

"A little heat?" Mary groaned. "In Florida? In the summer time? I think you're a sadist. What about the humidity? Think about the bugs!"

I thought about the bugs and how dumb girls are getting so hyper over them. And thinking about Mary screeching over every little one made me happier about not having the air on. I even thought how it wouldn't be that hard to help the bug population along some in her room.

"Ridiculous," Mom said, opening windows and doors that hadn't been opened since winter. "Why, my goodness!" she exclaimed, "There's even a little breeze blowing. Come over here stand by the door and you'll feel it."

"I'd break a sweat walking that far," Mary sighed, sitting not two feet away.

"I read somewhere that it costs more turning it off in the day and on again at night than leaving it running with the thermostat set a bit higher," Steve said. "Why don't we just put it up to eighty for a few days and see how it goes?"

"But I don't plan to turn it back on at night," Mom said, her voice going up along with her eyebrows. "I'm turning it off. O-F-F."

"Mo-om!" we all groaned.

"Not in August," Mary gasped. "We'll die in August."

"In that case," Mom said, "we won't have to worry about it, will we?"

Of course we lived through August and all the other months, too, without the A/C because like Mom said, "May, August, October. What's the difference? It's all the same here in Florida. Hot."

She's got that right. It's Sweat City all the way.

Anyway, after she got through with the air and she was sure nothing any of us was doing was costing money, like playing our stereos or watching TV - "It is OK if we breathe, isn't it?" Mary had wanted to know - she started clipping coupons out of the paper to save on food and walking to save on gas and sewing to save on clothes. And when she wasn't doing any of those things, she was trying to figure out other ways to save.

"She's getting to be a real pain in the ass with all this save, save, save," Mary complained one afternoon when Mom had gone off to the store with a wad of coupons big enough to choke a camel. "I'll gag if she cooks another one of those economy casseroles again tonight. We'd be better off eating cat food right out of the can."

"How about the Kool-Aid?" I said, sticking my tongue out for them to see. "Look, my tongue's permanently stained purple. We haven't even tasted Coke since Dad left."

We were staying cool the way we did every day, up to our necks in the bayou, swimming some, but mostly just hanging on to our old canoe floating upside down in the water.

"Yeah, well you'd worry about money, too, if you were her and had three kids to raise," Steve told Mary. "Especially if one of them was like you."

"Well, I wouldn't," Mary said. "Worry, I mean. I never saw worry solve anything. But if I was going to, I'd worry about my kids staying healthy without air conditioning and neat food. Not about money. Money's something you spend until it's gone. Then you can worry if you want. I mean, I just don't see the point."

"You don't see the point in anything," I told her, wondering how Steve could be so patient with her when what I wanted to do was smack her over the head with an oar.

"Shut your mouth," Mary said to me, and to Steve, "What I mean is, I don't mind being careful. Sort of... But shit, she doesn't have to make a career out of it, does she?"

"You've got to quit with the cussing," Steve told her, but he said it absent-mindedly, the way everybody does. Mary has cussed as long as I can remember. Mom says she must've been a sailor or a gangster in another life because she seems to have been born knowing all those words. Anyway, "Mom's scared," Steve went on. "Scared half to death."

"Don't talk dumb," I said, remembering all the things Mom had taught me not to be afraid of. "She's not scared of anything. She used to look under my bed for Dracula every night when I was a little kid. And once when I was with her she yelled at a cop!"

"Not your kind of scared, dummy," Steve said. "I'm talking adult scared."

"So tell us, Oh, Wise One," Mary sneered. "What's adult scared?"

"Adults are scared of things like financial ruin, dread diseases, major mechanical breakdowns that cost mega-bucks to fix. And of their kids," he looked sideways at Mary, "running amok. And then there's the IRS. And making all her own decisions. She's got to figure it all out by herself now."

Mary made a face and disappeared under the water, coming up far enough away that she wouldn't have to talk to us. Steve must've gotten to her though, because she went in earlier than usual that day and I heard the vacuum going and later horrendous crashing sounds that could only have meant she was emptying the dishwasher.

"The year of the big sweats," we call that year now. We even think it was funny. Weird how you laugh about stuff when it's history. While it was going on I don't remember a whole lot of laughing going on.

We didn't get a rainy season that year either. "Even God's dried up on us," Mary complained, helping me haul out our dirty bath water – after dark of course - so the plants out front wouldn't shrivel up and die and the neighbors get the idea we were broke. Usually, we get big storms late in the afternoons that time of year that cool things off and keep us green, but not that summer. So with the hot days and sticky nights and all the casseroles and Mom worrying, I was kind of looking forward to school starting up again. We all were.

Turned out Mom was looking forward to it, too.

"I probably won't be here when you kids get home today," she called out the day school started when we were all crashing around trying to remember where we'd dumped our school stuff back in June.

"Where will you be?" one of us called back.

"Out job hunting! I'm going to get one too. The paper's full of them. You just wait and see. Things are going to be a lot different around here. We'll turn the air back on."

"I'm coming straight home, taking my clothes off and lying down under the vent," Mary said, adding, "In my room, morons," when she saw Steve and me gagging.

"Maybe we'll even go out to dinner," Mom went on dreamily.

"How about a movie, too?" I suggested.

"Why not? A movie, too."

"Can we have cokes and popcorn?"

"Of course. Anything you want. Everything you want."

"Maybe she's human after all." Mary said.

"I am," Mom said, handing us each a lunch bag.

"You're ruining my image with these tacky bags, you know," Mary said, taking hers with a scowl.

"Sweetheart," Mom said, "an image as glorious as yours cannot possibly be ruined by a mere paper bag."

We were watching for her out the front window when she came home that day. We'd been there, waiting, since about four o'clock, showered, dressed-up, and ready to go.

"She didn't get a job," Steve said, watching her get out of her car and come up the front walk.

"Oh, shit!" Mary said. "That means no dinner, no movie, no damn nothing."

"How do you know?" I asked.

"Look at the way she's walking. Like she's going to a funeral. One of ours. Act like you don't notice."

"Hi, sweethearts. My, how nice you all look," Mom said, coming in the door with a big fake smile.

"How'd it go?" Steve asked.

"Oh, fine. Just fine."

"Cut the crap and tell it like it is," Mary snapped.

"Ma-ry," we all said, Steve and me mad, Mom with a sigh.

Mom kicked off her high heels and sort of folded into a chair. "It was awful," she sighed. "Just awful."

"How was it awful?"

"It was as bad-as-it-can-get awful. I'm unemployable. A nothing. Quite worthless, actually. I don't know how to do anything anymore. Nobody wants me." She made a prissy face, put on a squeaky voice and said, "I'm sorry, Mrs. Martin, but you've been away from the job market far too long to fill any of our present needs."

"Bunch of jerks!" Mary scowled.

"Like, what can't you do?" Steve asked. "I mean, there's got to be something out there you can do. Look at all the stuff you do around here."

"This has to have been the most humiliating day of my life," Mom went on with a shudder. "I felt so... inept. Useless. Like a bad joke. I thought I'd be able to get some kind of office job without even trying. After all, before I met your father I did work for a huge global company. You have to be pretty good to get that kind of job."

"See. You do know how to do something." Steve said. "Why didn't you go for that kind of job?"

"But I did! That's what makes it so humiliating. Everywhere I went I did just fine until it came to typing. But guess what? Surprise, surprise! They don't have typewriters anymore. They have computers... word processors... whatever... I didn't even know how to turn one on. Then, when they showed me, I somehow kept hitting the wrong key and everything I typed kept erasing itself. Poof! Gone! Oh, God! I was hopeless!"

She shrugged and tried another smile that didn't come off too good either. In fact it looked like she did it because what her face really wanted to do was cry.

"Eighteen years *is* too long to have been away from the job market," she went on. "So now I guess I have some catching up to do. I'll have to rent one of those awful computer things and learn how to use it. What upsets me most is that I wasted the whole summer. What was I thinking about?"

"How to save money," Mary said sourly.

"But I have to! Steve will be eighteen before we know it and ready for college. We've got to have more money."

"We'll make out fine, Mom," Steve said. "Stop worrying. Look at all the money I've made this summer mowing lawns and fixing docks. I can work and go to college too. Other people do it all the time."

"What's the big deal, Mom?" I asked. "We'll all turn eighteen one day."

"The big deal," she said with another awful smile, in fact the worst smile I'd ever seen in my life, "is that when each of you reach the age of eighteen, I lose your child support."

"Oh," we said. I mean, what else was there to say?

"Does this mean we can't go out to dinner and the movies?" Mary demanded to know, hands on her hips, mad as all. "Because I think this family deserves a break once in a while and I hurried home and did all the housework and I was hot as hell the whole time and I didn't start dinner because you said... You told us... And if you think I'm..."

"Mary, Mary," Mom said. "Calm down! We're going out to dinner. You're right. We do deserve a break. Just let me go change."

"How about the movies?" I called after her.

"You've got it," she called back. "Dinner. Movies. Cokes and popcorn. The whole nine yards."

"About damn time, too," Mary said, looking happy for the first time that whole entire summer.

Two

Next day a computer came into the house and was set up at the desk in the living room. "I always knew this room would come in handy for something," Mom said, pulling a chair up in front of what she called the "monster" and touching a key with one finger as though she thought it would haul off and bite her.

"Go in the kitchen please, Jeff, honey, and get me that little timer thing I use for baking," she told me, and when I came back with it she set it to go off in three minutes. "Three. Three's the magic number," she muttered.

"What's so magic about three?" I asked, pulling up a chair to watch.

"Sixty words a minute for three minutes used to be the criteria," she said, her fingers searching out the keys, "so that's what I'll give them. Darn..." she stopped and looked at what she'd done. I looked too.

"Did you mean to type that?" I asked, seeing rows and rows of h's and d's with a few x's thrown in here and there.

"What'd I tell you?" she said, hitting a key and watching in disbelief as everything she'd typed shrank itself to postage stamp size. "The thing's a monster. It has a mind of its own. All by itself it types a hundred words a minute, I bet, whereas my fingers, left alone, seem to type about ten. The trick is going to be synchronization. All I need is a little practice."

Practice. Practice. Coming home from school afternoons, there was Mom, typing away, the little bell on the timer dinging at three minute intervals.

"Sixty words a minute is all I need, " she'd moan as we came through the door, "and every time I get up to forty-five it takes on a life of its own. Mary... Sweetheart... I'm sorry but you're going to have to start dinner again tonight. I've just got to master this thing."

"Why me?" Mary'd scream, flinging down her books and settling in, hands on her hips, for a fight. "Do I look like a slave or something? What's the matter with these precious boys of yours? Are they paralyzed or something? Tell me!"

"Now, Mary," Mom soothed. "They're doing all the yard work and the repairs and the trash."

"Big damn deal! Once a week they shove the mower around and there's two of them!"

"Teach us to cook, Mom," Steve and I pleaded over and over again. "It's got to be easier than listening to her bitch."

"Can't you see I don't have time," she wailed. "I've got to practice. I have to master this thing."

Gradually though, without her ever leaving her desk, we learned to cook.

"What's the difference between smoke and steam?" we'd call through to her. And, "What does it look like now?" she'd yell through to us. So we'd carry stuff into the living room, right in the pot, and she'd take a look and say turn the heat up a little - or down, whichever - and give it a few more minutes and had we read the directions? That always helped. It wasn't long before we got to where we were serving up some pretty decent food.

Meantime, in spite of the hours Mom was spending at the monster, she didn't make any headway at all. It got so that the sight of her hunched at the desk became such a part of our lives that for months afterwards I'd think I still saw her there when I walked past the living room and even today, when I see someone at a computer, I get a sick kind of feeling in my stomach.

"She's too intense," Steve told me when I asked how come she still hadn't licked it after two months. "She's trying too hard. All she's doing is sit there practicing mistakes. Getting real good at them."

To her, I heard him say, "Come on, Mom, give it a rest. You're pushing yourself too hard. And what's worse, you're not believing in yourself. It's really not that hard. Besides, the world isn't going to end if you don't get the hang of it."

"Our world will," she'd say, looking like it already had. "I just can't get them together, you know. The speed and all those crazy keys that put stuff up on the screen I don't know how to get rid of. I can do one or the other. Not both."

"So how did you get that job before you got married?" he asked.

"It was different then," she sighed. "I was young and single. I didn't feel any pressure. In fact, I'm ashamed to admit it, but I believe I was arrogant enough to think I was doing everyone a favor working for them. And I don't recall ever being asked to take a typing test. It was all about shorthand in those days. Besides, nobody'd ever heard of computers back then. Too bad some fool had to come along and invent them. But don't worry. I'll get a job soon. By Christmas, at least."

In November, when she realized what we'd known all along, that she wasn't getting anywhere, she said, "Guess what I've been thinking?"

Nobody wanted to ask. You never knew what Mom was thinking.

"I've been thinking I could really get the hang of this computer business if I went to night school. Somebody there is bound to be able to help me."

"You'd think so," Mary said. "It's what you'll be paying them for, isn't it?"

"You wouldn't mind too terribly much, would you, Jeff, honey?" Mom asked me.

"Why would I mind?"

"Well... Because you're the youngest and you need a mother at home more than Steve and Mary."

"Oh, my God," Mary sighed, looking wearily at the ceiling. "Here she goes on another one of her Mother-of-the-Year kicks. He's going to be twelve soon, Mom. I was already baby-sitting when I was eleven, remember? What are you going to do? Stay home and pick up his smelly socks? Give us a break." She turned to me. "You don't have to worry, little dinkums. I'll chase the spooks out from under your bed every night, I promise. And if you're extra good I might even sing you a lullaby."

"So is it OK with you?" Mom asked me again, ignoring Mary.

To Mary I said, "Shut your mouth." And to Mom, "I'm not a little kid."

"I mind," Steve said, which surprised me so much I settled the front legs of the chair I was sitting in back down on the floor nice and easy, so I wouldn't fall off it. "Not for us," he went on, "but for you. You shouldn't have to go out to night school and you don't belong in an office. It's not your style. It's... Well, I think you're short-changing yourself. You could do much better if only you'd..."

"Short-changing myself?" Mom interrupted with a gasp, and I remember thinking it was a good thing she was standing at the time because she certainly would have fallen out of any chair she might have been sitting in. As it was, she pushed herself away from the kitchen counter and I thought she was going to get really mad, but she didn't. She laughed. What you might call a hollow laugh, but definitely a laugh.

"Whatever else I might be doing, sweetheart, I assure you I'm not short-changing myself. I'm accepting the situation I'm in and doing what has to be done, that's all. Starting all over again at the bottom just happens to be part of it and I'll just have to swallow my pride and make the best of things."

I had to smile to myself writing that just now. Mom sure changed a lot over the next few years and she doesn't like being reminded of how she used to be: a scared-to-death ninny with zero self-confidence. "What a pitiful wimp I was in those days," she sighs. But back then, that's the way she was.

Four nights a week then, we'd eat early and she'd take off for night school and you know something? We loved having her out of the house like that. We'd watch the headlights of her car sweep across the dark living room as she backed out and headed up the street and then we'd dive for the TV and the stereo and blast both and Mary'd get going with the popcorn.

"I can't believe she's not here," I'd sigh with relief.

"I can't believe we're not listening to her cussing out that computer," Steve said. "It's like you get up in the morning and what's the first thing you see? Mom looking worried. You come home from school and what do you see?"

"Mom. Looking frantic," I said.

"Right." Steve said. "And last thing at night?"

"Mom. Looking desperate."

"It could be worse. Think if it was a piano she was crashing around on in there," Mary said at the same time she was tossing burnt kernels in the sink and turning on the garbage disposal.

Before the giggle in my throat got past the popcorn in my mouth there was a horrendous noise and kernels and water both were coming off the ceiling.

"Oh, shit! Oh, God!" Mary gasped.

"Turn it off, moron!" Steve yelled trying to get around the counter.

"You're such a dumb bitch," I muttered, choking.

By then, Steve had elbowed Mary aside and turned the disposal off and we were looking at the mess dripping off the ceiling. "I don't know," he muttered doubtfully, flicking the then-dead switch of the disposal, "I don't think I know enough to fix it."

"What do you mean, you don't know enough to fix it?" Mary screamed. "You've got to fix it. Else she'll have us chewing garbage every night with our teeth."

He fixed it.

I guess night school must've done what it was supposed to do because right after Christmas Mom started going out on interviews again and one cold January afternoon - cold for Florida, that is, in the sixties - the sky a clear, pale blue and the sun a distant, kindly relative to the one that fries us in summer, we heard her come in, her high heels clattering across the slate entry hall. We were all in the den, Steve and me doing homework, Mary sighing over some far-out clothes in a fashion magazine, which makes me think that in all the years we were growing up, I never once saw Mary doing homework. But anyway, in comes Mom, all excited and happy looking.

"Turn the crap music off," she said, but not in a mad way. And then she turned the TV off herself and stood in front of it with the first really big smile we'd seen on her face since the divorce.

"Guess what?" she asked.

"Why do you call it crap music?" I wondered out loud.

"Don't ask!" Mary yelped.

"Because..." Mom began. "Well, to me it sounds the way one of those paintings on black velvet would sound. If it had a sound, that is."

"Yeah?" I said, wondering.

"Hmmm..." Steve said, "And how...?"

"I told you idiots, don't ask!" Mary snapped. "You honest-to-God do not want to know."

"All noise and no sound," Mom said. "Just like the paintings. You know, all color and no light."

"I told you jerks not to ask," Mary said. "You should listen to me."

"Never mind that now," Mom said. "Guess what?"

"You got a job," we said.

"Yes, I did. In some law offices. I start Monday. How'd you guess?"

"We're smart kids," Mary said.

"Yes, you are. Why not? I'm your mother. Go get showered and changed. We're going out to dinner. This old bread winner's going to win some bread so tonight we get to spend some."

She didn't have to tell us twice. We were out of that room like it was on fire and I guess Mom was too excited to settle down and wait for us because she followed us and paced around outside our closed bedroom doors yelling about all the stuff she was going to do now she'd be earning money.

"We'll run the air this summer," she screamed.

I heard Mary give a loud "Humph!" and Mom saying, "Yes, really. I promise." And then she was outside my door yelling about how she'd be able to let me take scuba lessons and get certified and then she was hollering at Steve's saying how easy it was going to be for her to put him through college.

You'd have thought she'd have run out of cool stuff to tell us about by the time we were all back out there with her, but she kept it up all the way to the restaurant where she made us order the most expensive things on the menu even though I'd rather have had a burger. She got us all so caught up in our future that by the time we'd finished eating and she'd drunk a glass of wine, we were all educated, had traded the car, were wearing new clothes, had the house painted inside and out and were even considering a maid. One who'd stay and fix dinner. It was fun. I loved sitting there listening to her talk about all the things we could do for a change instead of what we couldn't. And seeing her looking happy for once. Even Mary got caught up in it and forgot to cuss and criticize everything but it was her who thought to ask Mom how much she'd be earning.

"Minimum wage, darling. Of course. One has to start somewhere," Mom said airily. "But don't worry. I'll get raises. Lots of them. Why in no time at all, I'll be..."

"Yeah, we know," Mary glowered. "Driving a Jaguar."

"Mary," Mom sort of sighed, trying to look stern and dignified which wasn't easy on account of the wine, "Shut up, OK? I'm on my way. Don't knock me down before I even get up, all right?"

For once in her life Mary looked ashamed of herself and managed to keep her smart-ass remarks to herself for the rest of the evening.

Mom's mood lasted through the rest of that week and into Sunday afternoon and then she quieted down and the worry lines were back.

Monday morning she was a mess. I mean, a walking disaster.

"Ready to kick ass, Mom?" Mary asked.

"What a terrible expression," Mom shuddered, sitting down at the breakfast table. "Actually, I didn't sleep too well. And... um... I don't seem to be able to eat too well either, do I?" she went on, looking woefully at a piece of toast she'd picked up and put down so many times it had disintegrated into a pile of crumbs.

"There's something I never told any of you," she whispered, giving up trying to eat at all and looking as though she were about to burst into tears.

"What?" we whispered back, scared half to death to hear her answer.

"I... I still don't know how to work a computer. Not really."

Mary started laughing like a lunatic. "Oh, yes you do! Else how did you pass their stupid test?"

"They didn't give me one." Mom said, eyes downcast. "They just asked was I 'computer friendly' and I said yes."

"See," I said. "They don't even care."

"Oh, but they do." Mom moaned. "Trust me. They do."

"Tell them you're not into computers," Mary said. "You know, like maids who aren't into windows. Or tell them you've always had a personal preference for cursive."

"Listen, Mom," Steve said. "Look at me. Read my lips. YOU CAN TOO USE A COMPUTER. You've just got to believe it. And in yourself..."

"Wing it," Mary advised. "Stare 'em down. And if they don't like it, tell 'em where to shove it. I don't see any problems myself."

Mom gulped. "Hand me down the Pepto Bismol," she said to me. "My stomach doesn't feel any too secure."

By the time we trailed her out to the car, she'd swallowed half the bottle and said she was feeling better, but a fool could tell she was lying. She looked even worse than she had at the breakfast table. Terrified was what she was.

"Be cool," Steve told her, his arm around her shoulder. "You know you can hack it. It's just a crummy job."

"I know I can," she said mournfully, climbing into the car like it was a hearse. "But I hate going off and leaving you all. I really do. I don't believe in working moms, you know. I belong here at home with you."

"We're not going to be home, remember?" Mary said. "We go to school. All day long."

"Yes, I know..." her voice trailed off and she looked at herself in the rearview mirror. "You don't think I look..." she paused, "too old?"

"Too old?" we asked, not getting her meaning.

"Yes. Old. You know, over the hill. Wrinkles, sags, gray hair. Maybe just a tad, um... plump?" She tried buttoning the buttons of the suit jacket she had on and there was no way they were going to close. "Youth's the thing nowadays, you know. All the other women in that place look as young and skinny as Mary."

"You look great."

"Fantastic!"

"Like a kid!"

"I love you all," Mom said. "I really do. You know that. And please remember, I'm not doing this for a career or anything. I'm not a Libber."

"Will you go," Mary begged. "You're getting so boring."

I'll say this for Mary. She's bossy and obnoxious most of the time, but when one of us needs a good hard shove to do something we don't want to do, you can count on her being there to do the shoving.

"I'm going, dammit, " Mom said, straightening suddenly and looking all business. "Gonna go for the gold!"

THREE

"To think how I worried about that stupid computer and nearly drove us all crazy over my jobs," Mom was to say after her "career" days were over.

Easy words for her then but it took her years to know it.

"We kept telling you," I reminded her.

"I know it," she said. "But I guess I had to go through it in my own way. At least now I know how not to be. What a pitiful, insecure, sheltered little ninny I was back then."

"You were a mess," I agreed.

"Still, those years were the best thing that ever happened to me."

"They were?"

"Of course they were. Think about it, Jeff! Suppose there had never been a divorce and I was still married to your father. I would never have been pushed to do anything. Not that I made any great contributions to humanity out there in the world, but at least I was out there and I began to come to terms with myself. It gives me a nice secure feeling only, of course, if I ever had to do it again I'd go out there expecting nice things to happen and so they would."

"Of course," I said.

"I wish I had been even tougher on myself and the world this last time out but at least I was tough enough to earn a living and pay our bills and help Steve get himself through college. What if I had just spent those years at home? Look at what I'd have missed. Look at what you'd have missed!"

"I'd have missed?"

"Not just you. All of you. You'd be useless. I'd be useless. I would have spent all those years waiting on all of you, doing things for you that you should have been doing for yourselves. Putting all of you first and then, when you grew up and left, I'd have probably sulked around, wallowing in self pity, saying, 'What about me?' And, 'After all I did for them...' And you, you wouldn't know how to cook or clean or iron a shirt or sew on a button. You wouldn't have learned a single useful thing."

"Like it really makes a difference knowing that stuff," I said.

"It's not knowing 'that stuff' that matters. It's being self-reliant. Besides, you did something much more important than that."

"Like what?"

"Like helping your Mother grow up. Teaching her to stand on her own two feet."

"Yeah," I said. "That was the tough part. You were impossible."

"Now I know what a mother feels like the first day her kid goes off to kindergarten," Mary said, the evening of the day Mom started her first job. Dinner was cooking in the oven, the table was set and we were waiting for her to get home.

"I hope she hacked it," Steve sighed, his big toes busy again making patterns in the shag. "Man, I can't take another day like today. I couldn't think straight worrying about her. Bet I get an 'F' in calculus."

"She's coming," I said, seeing her old car rumbling up the driveway.

"What's she look like?" Steve asked, coming up behind me.

"She's smiling."

"Only because she knows we're watching," Mary said. "Any fool can smile. Did she kick butt or did they kick hers? That's what we need to know."

"I feel as though I've been away for a year," Mom said, coming in and kissing us. "I'm surprised you haven't all grown at least an inch while I was gone. Is that dinner that smells so good?"

"All right, Mom," Mary said. "Cut the small talk and tell it like it is."

"I'll small talk you all evening, Mary, if you don't stop being so bossy. I'm a wage earner now. Show a little respect." Wearily, she stepped out of her shoes and flopped on the couch. "They ought to pay me just for wearing heels all day," she moaned. "I think I'm going to be a clock watcher," she went on, her eyes shut. "This has to have been the longest day I ever lived through. I felt like I was in jail. Those libbers must be crazy thinking jobs mean freedom. Housewives have freedom. I think it's me though, not the job. I must've become too independent over the years."

"You don't seem any too independent to me," Mary said.

"Shut up and let her finish," Steve said to Mary. "Go on, Mom."

"Where to begin? I felt like I was in a dream. I mean, I couldn't believe it was really me in there. It was as though I was playing a role. And I was homesick. I really was. And I don't know about the man I work for. He's pretty awful. He made me type every letter over because he said I'd made the text too narrow. Said it looked like a newspaper column. I was mortified. But the women there are all very nice and helpful. They call my boss "The Swine" behind his back. No wonder. And I already heard him call me 'the Mommy' behind mine. As though being a mother is something to sneer at."

"You should quit." Mary said flatly. "Like, right now."

"Quit?" Mom gasped, her eyes flying open. "Dear God, Mary, where did I go wrong with you? I haven't even begun."

"Well, give it a week maybe but if the guy's calling you names your first day, I say quit. It can only go downhill."

"You worry me, Mary. You really do. I can't imagine how you're going to adjust when you get out in the world. You can't quit a job the day you start it. What if everyone did that? You have to have some sense of commitment. Is it just you, I wonder, or your whole generation?"

Mary shrugged. "Why take a year to do what's obvious the first day?"

"I told you why. Because it's me, not the job. I just have to readjust, learn to take orders again. Be a 'team' player, as the Swine puts it. Give me time. I just wish I worked for a nicer man. Maybe I've turned into a man hater, too."

"Tell us more about this guy," Mary said, and when Mom hesitated, trying to find the words to describe him, hurried on with, "Go on, tell us. I'm an expert on men. I'll tell you how to straighten him out."

"I'm sure you would, Mary. But he does pay my salary and your tactics, like shooting him a bird or telling him where to shove it, wouldn't go over too well. This is the business world I'm in. Not high school."

"At least he'd know how you feel about him."

"Yes, he would. And I'd know how he felt about me. From outside on the sidewalk."

"Come on, Mom. Don't let her sidetrack you with all her expertise," Steve said. "Tell us what he's like."

"Well... he's gross. Slovenly. He loves the sound of his own voice. He flits around on the balls of his feet simpering to his clients. But to us, "his girls" as he calls us, he's snide. Borderline crude. And he's unorganized to the point his file cabinets are empty and you have to crawl around on the floor to find stuff. Plus he wears rings. Can you imagine that? Diamond rings. Four of them. Ugh! Enough! Let's eat. I'll get used to it. Just give me time."

Well, she had her time. Five years of it. And it took her all of them to realize it wasn't the jobs bringing her down. Or the bosses. It was herself. She was her own worst enemy.

Like, I remember one weekend afternoon when we were all messing around swimming and having a good time and then Mom pulls herself out of the water and sits on the seawall and before you know it she's looking miserable.

"All right," Mary said, pulling herself up beside her. "What is it? You can tell me."

"Tomorrow's Monday," Mom said. "That's what it is. It's like... Well, there's work and there's home and I don't ever seem to get them prioritized. When I'm in the office I feel guilty because I'm not at home and when I'm home I feel guilty because I can't get excited over their little legal frenzies. But really! Twenty legal pages to tell someone to move a fence post two inches? Who cares? And who needs it? Especially at five o'clock when I'm supposed to be on my way home."

"It serves you right," Mary said. "If five o'clock is quitting time, then quit. You let them dump on you. Either get tough or get another job."

"I need that job, Mary," Mom said, all indignant. "I'm not out there to see who's toughest. I've told you, it's me. I have to change. Bend. Be more flexible. Work late if I have to. I mean... They could fire me!"

"No wonder the women of your generation need liberating," Mary sneered. "You put up with too much shit as it is and now you're going to smile and try harder? Get real!"

By then, Steve and I were on the seawall, too, and Steve said, "Mary's right, Mom. You should quit. That guy you work for sounds like a real jerk. You got a bad break, that's all. Start over. And next time, stick up for yourself."

"I'm not quitting," Mom howled. "Not after what I went through to get that job. I'm lucky to be working at all with my inexperience. Beggars can't be choosers."

"You're pathetic," Mary said.

Mary was right. She was pathetic. I mean, getting her to stand on her own two feet was like pushing a stalled Mack truck up a steep hill and it took a lot of patience from all of us to make it happen. Like the time she was really sick with the 'flu and still planning on going in.

"What is it makes you think you're so damn important the world will end if you don't show?" Steve asked, watching her weave around the kitchen.

"But that's just it!" Mom wailed. "I'm not important. If I don't go in they might realize they can get along just fine without me. They'll give my responsibilities to someone else. Maybe permanently."

"Leave her alone," Mary said with disgust. "You can see she loves playing the martyr. Let her."

"Be for real, Mom," I said. "Go back to bed."

"No! I'm going in. We need the money. I need the experience. Besides, they frown on sick days."

"So they frown," Steve said. "Let 'em. And screw money and experience. It's more important that you believe in yourself. You're sick. Go back to bed."

You could see Mom starting to waver. "Do you really think so?" she said. "Maybe just this once then. I do feel so awful. Call in for me, will you? Tell them I'm very contagious."

"When I start work," Mary said, watching Mom totter back to bed, "I'm taking off at least one day a month whether I'm sick or not."

"You, I hope they do kick out," Steve said. "On your first day."

When we got home from school that day, Mom was sitting up in bed looking better and she said, "I've been lying here all day thinking maybe I should go into real estate. I mean, this is Florida. Land is booming. All the women I know selling real estate are making fortunes. They drive around in Mercedes and wear designer clothes. And they don't have to mess with computers. What do you think?"

"I think it sounds great," Steve said. "When can you start?"

"I like the part about the clothes and the Mercedes," Mary said. "Go for it."

"I'd have to take courses," Mom said. "Go to night school. Pass exams. Spend money. There'll be no income at first. You only get commissions. What do you think, Jeff?"

"We've been through this once already, Mom. Stop treating me like a dopey little kid."

"Maybe I'll do it," Mom said. "I just might."

So instead of a computer in the living room, we got books on real estate all over the house and one night a week Mom was going straight from work to real estate classes.

As her exam got closer, it got so you never saw her without a book. She'd bring them to the dinner table and eat with them propped up in front of her and every once in a while, when our squabbling got bad enough, she'd look up and say things like, "I'm sorry sweeties, what was that you said?" Or, "I'm sorry... Dinner time should be your time. They say the family that eats together, stays together. Do you have any problems? Things you'd like to talk to me about? You know you all come first." And when we'd shake our heads, no, she'd say, "Good. You know I'm here if you need me but the state exam is next Monday. Mary, it's your turn to quiz me. Start on page eighty-seven."

"This is getting old, Mom." Mary groaned. "I know this stuff better than you do. Want me to take the exam for you?"

"Oh, I only wish you could!" Mom sighed.

When she finally got home from taking her exam we heard her go straight to the hall closet and dump all her real estate books in its farthest corner.

"Did you ace it?" Steve called.

"I've no idea," she said, coming into the room. "All I know is I'm glad it's over. That and the night school. No more of that for me, ever, thank you kindly. Have you all done your homework? You better. You don't want to have to go back to school in mid-life like me. It's the pits."

"Thanks for the tip, Mom," Mary said. "But we already got the message. Watching you'd turn anybody off."

"When will you know if you passed?" Steve asked.

"Three weeks, they said. Watch it take five."

When the letter finally came, she was scared to open it. Steve was in the bathroom showering at the time and she pushed it under the door yelling, "Open it for me, please," and then paced around outside the door.

When Steve came out, he steered Mom to a chair and said, "You better sit down for this. Are you ready?"

Mom nodded.

"You passed."

Mom sighed. "I knew it. I must've missed the question on acreage. I... Wait a minute. What did you say?"

"I said, you passed."

Old Mom was out of that chair in a bound screeching like she'd seen a rattle snake.

"It was my coaching," Mary said. "Let's go pick up that Mercedes."

"Of course," Mom said. "But not right away. First..." And she's looking all worried again. "First... Well... Now I'm going to have to quit my job!"

"Wasn't that the whole point?" Mary spluttered.

"I guess," Mom said, looking like her life raft had sprung a leak.

"You're pitiful, Mom," Mary said and looking at our three faces, Mom could see that for once Steve and I agreed with her.

A couple of days later, she came home, looked at herself in the hall mirror with a pleased kind of smile, and said, "I did it. I quit!"

"Way to go!" Steve and I said, each giving her a high five.

"It took you long enough," Mary glowered.

"Let's go downtown tomorrow and throw cream pies at The Swine," I said, "You know, like they do on TV."

"Right when he's coming down the courthouse steps all puffed up with self-importance because he's just evicted a poor family from a hovel," Mom said dreamily. Then, "No. If anybody needs a cream pie in the face, it's me. I should have listened to all of you and left the day I started, just like Mary said. And I want you all to promise me one thing. Promise me you'll never, ever be attorneys. I'd die of shame if I thought I'd spawned another one on this earth."

Over the years she made us promise the same for every job she ever had so as well as not being attorneys, we've sworn not to be architects, interior decorators or real estate brokers. And that's OK. None of us wanted to be any of those things anyway.

"Listen to her, will you," Mary said. "She's finally telling it like it is."

"It's a beginning," Steve said.

"The beginning of what?" I asked.

"Of being herself. Right here, folks. Before our very eyes!"

"Oh, God," Mom said, ruining it all. "I hope I did the right thing. No more paychecks. No more benefits. We'll have to turn the air off again. Eat more casseroles. Steve's college is getting closer. What if... What if I don't make it in real estate?"

"What if?" Mary said, grabbing her by the shoulders. "What if you do make it, huh? Make it big? Did you ever stop to think about that?"

F OUR

I guess the kindest thing to say about Mom's career in real estate is not too much. She got herself chased by dogs trying to get people to list their homes with her company; watched her associates rack up million dollar sales with one phone call; had clients she worked with for weeks buy from competitors. And then there came the day she was showing a vacant house to a retired couple. She'd just finished showing them the upstairs, was standing in the entry hall downstairs talking to the old guy, when they hear this creaking and cracking from the stairwell and before they can do a thing about it, they see the old lady sinking up to her knees through the termite ridden wood of the third step up from the bottom.

'Course while she's telling us all this she's crying her eyes out and Mary's rolling around on the couch laughing like a hyena.

"It's not a laughing matter, Mary," Mom sobbed. "It was humiliating. I had to go next door and call the Rescue Squad and even they had a terrible time pulling her out. And then my Broker showed up and acted as if it was all my fault. Then the old couple got nasty and said they were going to sue me. You should have heard the things they called me! Words even you don't know, Mary."

"Want to bet?" Mary smirked.

Mom let out a long sigh, part of it, I think, for Mary and part for the old couple, and said, "Well, that's it. Face it. I'm jinxed. I've put a million miles on the car. Knocked on doors till my knuckles bled. Sat on every Open House in town. Talked on the phone till I lost my voice. To say nothing of the money I've spent. All our reserves are gone. We're broke. It's over."

"Don't talk like that," Steve said. "You've just hit a rough spot. Things'll get better. You can't quit now."

"I already have," Mom said. "It's done. My broker congratulated me on a wise decision. I should have known I couldn't do it."

"So now what?" Steve wanted to know.

"Back to an office, I guess," Mom said, looking uncertain. "What else? I heard about an opening in an architectural firm."

Mary groaned. "Oh, God. Not that again, Mom. Don't you see it's not the jobs? It's you. You don't believe in yourself. You don't assert yourself."

"I'm sorry, Mary. I tried. I really did. I wanted you all to be so proud of me. I'm just not tough like you. I guess I'm something of a wimp."

"Yes, you are." Mary agreed. "Don't know why we still love you like we do. Can't help ourselves, I guess."

"I don't know why. I seem to be pretty useless."

"That's enough, Mom," Mary glowered. "Knock it off. A little self-pity goes a long way. You're not a wimp here at home. Ask us! So how come you fall apart out there? What you got to do is put on an act. You got to act like you know exactly what you're doing... Where you're going... Like nobody better get in your way. Nothing's stopping you. Just you."

"But that's just it. I don't know how to think about what I want or where I'm going, never mind act it out," Mom said. "How could I when I was raised to believe it was my *duty* to put everybody else in the world first? That it was positively wicked to do otherwise? Why, my whole life's been about what other people want. My parents. Your father. You kids. My boss. My broker. Plus all those other authority figures I was taught to respect and obey. You know, the teachers, the priests, the doctors, the government. How can I possibly have any idea what I want when all of the above have told me I couldn't have it anyway. Maybe I'm at the point where I don't even have a 'self' anymore."

"Watch it, guys," Mary warned. "Sounds to me like we've got a full blown identity crisis coming on here."

"An identity crisis," Mom repeated kind of wonderingly. "Do you suppose that's what it could be? You mean I could maybe get a better handle on things if I figured out who I was and what I want to do first, and then...?"

"That's what we've been trying to tell you all along." Steve said.

"Yeah," I said. "We keep telling you."

"I don't know," Mom said doubtfully. "Where would I begin? I mean, where I came from, putting yourself first was considered downright selfish."

"Yeah, well look where it got you," Mary said. "Zero self esteem. Insecure. Scared to take a stand on anything. Bombing out on jobs. Hooked on Pepto Bismol..."

Mom sighed. A real gut wrencher. "How come you all seem so much wiser than me?" she asked.

"Yeah," I said. "How come most of the time I feel like it's us the adults and you the kid?"

"Oh, Lord," Mom gulped. "Am I really so bad that even you, the youngest, knows more about life than me?"

"It's OK, Mom," Steve said. "Don't go into a tailspin over it. You're catching on. There's a self in there somewhere. You just need to find it."

"I guess..." Mom said doubtfully. "I can see I'm going to have to make some changes. But... where will I begin?"

"Just about every place, I'd say," Mary said pityingly.

"I... I think I'll just go think this all through quietly. On my own..." Mom said, getting up and heading for her room.

Half an hour later we hear the door open and she's back. Only she doesn't look like Mom at all. She's put on a lot of make up and fixed her hair so it looks kind of... puffy? And she's put together an outfit that's... well, weird.

"Well, say something," she coaxed after a few minutes of total silence from us. "I... I thought if I started with how I look... You know, maybe tried for a more assertive appearance, it'd be a start."

To me, Steve hissed, "Keep your mouth shut!" and to Mom, "You look, uh, really... Really different."

"Going out hooking, Mom?" Mary asked.

Mom kind of gulped and ran out of the room while Steve and I turned on Mary, ready to really let her have it.

"Don't look at me," she warned before we could open our mouths.

"You're the one told her she had to change," Steve accused.

"Yeah. Change. Not freak."

We'd just gotten back into our homework when we hear the door open again and Mom's back. This time she's got on a big baggy sweater, a skirt that comes down to her ankles, flat shoes and all the puffy hair's been pulled back into a big bow. A big, puffy bow.

"How about this?" Mom asks, twirling in front of us. "Is this better? More subtle? The book says it's right for all types and all ages."

"Looks more like Little Bo-Peep to me," Mary said. "Can I borrow it for Halloween?"

Mom turned her back on Mary and looked at Steve and me.

"Sorry, Mom," Steve said. "It's getting better but you're not there yet."

"What's the matter with the way you always look?" I asked, and right away I had Steve and Mary glaring at me and Mom leaving the room in a big hurry again and then Mary's loading herself up with magazines and following after her. Then both she and Mom headed back to Mary's room and that's how it went till nearly bed time: back and forth and to and fro and talk, talk, talk with Steve and me keeping our heads low, staying out of it, until we heard Mary clear her throat and say, "Ladies and Jerks," in a loud voice and she was leading Mom towards us dressed in a mix of both their clothes.

"Holy shit! Oops... Sorry, Mom. But hey! You look terrific!" Steve said.

"Yeah! Wow!" I said. "Now I see what you meant earlier. You did look a wreck." And from the looks I'm getting from Steve and Mary, I know I've done it again. Said the wrong thing.

"That's OK, honey," Mom said. "I did look a wreck. I hadn't realized. But now, thanks to Mary, I'm ready to take on the world." She broke off, seeing Mary headed for the garage with an armload of her clothes. "Just leave them all, honey," she called. "I'll hang them back up in a minute. And thanks again, sweetheart. I don't know what I'd do without you."

"Me, either," Mary said. "But remember what I told you, changing the outside's the easy part. The tough part's going to be changing the inside and you're going to have to do that all by yourself. You're gonna have to learn to live up to this gorgeous new outside. Show 'em you're somebody they can't mess with." She gave the clothes she was carrying a heave, gathering up dangling sleeves and belts, and went on, "And these aren't hanging back up, they're going out, OK? O.U.T."

"But, Mary! What'll I wear? My closet's empty!"

"We'll figure something," Mary said, tossing them into the garage. "But these are going to Goodwill else first time I turn my back, you'll be wearing them again, looking like you used to look. I know you."

Well, like Mary said, changing the outside was the easy part. I mean, seeing Mom leave for work next day looking like a really cool new person, who'd have guessed nothing had really changed? Not me.

"Where've you been?" Mary, looking madder than all, wanted to know when Mom came in after seven that night.

"I'm really sorry I'm so late." Mom said, all flustered. "Did you all eat?"

"Steve served up some kind of slop at six," Mary said. "Where were you?"

"Oh..." Mom was evasive. "I had a few errands to run. And I got stuck in traffic. You wouldn't believe the traffic out there tonight. Where is Steve?"

"At basketball practice. He had to bum a ride. Where were you?"

"I told you. I had errands to run. The cleaners. And I had to stop off at the supermarket," Mom babbled. "And then I ran into Becky and you know how she talks."

But Mary wasn't about to let her off the hook. "You're lying, Mom. You let that creep boss of yours keep you late again, didn't you?"

"Now, Mary..." Mom began.

"I knew it," Mary interrupted, sounding really defeated. "This whole new outside's just a total waste of time. It was supposed to give you some self-confidence, make you feel worthy, more assertive. But nothing's changed. You're still scared to death inside."

"Mary, try to understand. It's not that simple. I had the boss on the phone fit to be tied 'till way past five. He was calling from one of our sites. The painters had done the whole house in peach when he'd ordered pink. And the landscapers had put in northern plantings when the clients specifically wanted tropical. It took forever to get it all straightened out."

"That's no excuse," Mary said. "You should've told him..."

But now it was Mom who interrupted, snapping. "Look, Mary, I still haven't paid the dentist. Steve starts college next fall. The car insurance is due. Get off my back. I did what I had to do."

Scowling, Mary got up and left the room.

"If you talked to your boss, just once, like you just talked to Mary," I said. "You might start getting some place."

"Rome wasn't built in a day," Mom sighed. "I'm trying. Look, I even checked out some books from the library in my lunch hour." She upended the bag she'd been carrying, spilling books on the counter.

She had four. All of their titles beginning, *How to...*

"You think they'll help?" I asked.

"Of course. Otherwise I wouldn't have wasted my time. All knowledge is in books, you know. And these are written by experts." She picked up, *How to be Assertive and Get More Out of Life.* "I'll start with this one. Let's see, if I read a couple of chapters a night, I'll have myself turned around in no time. Maybe even by the weekend."

We didn't have to wait till the weekend. Next morning, just when we were finishing our cereal, Mom comes striding out of her room looking fiercer than a drill instructor I saw in a movie one time.

"Jeff!" she starts with me. "Sit up straight and get your elbows off the table when you eat. Steve! I want that yard mowed the minute you get home from school. Today. And Mary! I insist you vacuum before school. Not after. After school is for homework."

"I wasn't eating," I said. "I finished a long time ago."

"I mowed yesterday," Steve said. "After school and before practice. Go take a look."

Mary didn't say anything. Just took Mom by the arm, steered her around the counter, and with a pained look, pointed to the carpet which clearly bore the marks of a thorough vacuuming.

"Oh..." Mom faltered. "I must've been in the shower. I didn't hear." She straightened, put the fierce look back in place and said. "That's as it should be. See you keep it up. Have a good day. Anybody gets in your way, kick 'em under the rug. Dinner tonight is at six. Sharp! Be here."

"What's with her?" Steve asked, when the sound of the garage door closing behind her had died away.

"It's the book," I said.

"It'll pass." Mary said.

"What's its title?" Steve wondered out loud. "*How to Make Enemies Every Time You Open Your Mouth?* Jeez... Hey! Did I tell you Dad's getting married again?"

"There's another one needs straightening out," Mary sighed. "Man, what a screwed-up generation."

"Tell you one thing," Steve said. "Mom's not gonna have a very good day walking around with that kind of attitude."

She didn't. Have a good day, I mean. She said things started going wrong as soon as she stopped in for gas on her way to work and Chuck, the station owner, told her he'd be with her in a minute. Right off and flat out Mom told him "In a minute" wasn't going to cut it with her anymore and she'd take her business elsewhere.

"Is that how come you came limping in here just now with a broken heel?" Mary wanted to know.

"Yes," Mom sighed. "Wouldn't you know I ran completely dry two blocks from the office and had to hoof it. And then when I finally walked in there's the boss looking at the clock instead of me, saying in that smarmy way of his, 'A little late today aren't we, dearie? Is there a problem?'"

"What'd you tell him," Mary urged her on.

"I told him I didn't have problems anymore. That I controlled my own destiny."

"Oh, brother," Steve sighed. "You're really..."

"I know. I know." Mom stopped him. "I've realized aggression is not my style. I didn't like the way I sounded. So grating! So rude! So harsh! But this," she pulled a book from her briefcase, "seems much more me and just as effective. I leafed through it briefly. It's about how if you're peaceful within, why, you just naturally become stronger, more confident, without."

The book's title was something about inner peace and had a picture of an Indian guru staring at a candle on the cover.

"I saw that guy on a TV talk show," Mary yelped. "The whole set nearly went up in flames when the candle fell over. He didn't act any too peaceful then, I tell you what. They had to cut to a commercial."

"You just made that up," I said.

"So!" she hissed. "You want her lighting candles all over the place and then going into a trance like that Indian guy does?"

"I'll skip the candle part," Mom said. "We don't have any anyway and I want to give it a few minutes right now. I'll just stare at a crystal and do some chanting and then I'll fix us a nice little dinner. Harmoniously. Peacefully. All answers, all knowledge, comes from within, you know."

"Meditation is definitely the answer," she said later at the dinner table, her voice pitched very low. "Just think, I've only been at it half an hour and already I know how to put Steve through college." She looked at us expectantly.

"OK," Steve said. "I'll take the bait. How?"

Mom smiled gently, like Mona Lisa, and said, "Why... one semester at a time."

"Is there any other way?" Mary asked. "I mean, that's all the kid can handle, isn't it? One semester at a time?"

Mom chuckled softly. "Of course." She turned to Steve. "The whole secret is not to think of it in terms of a large, unwieldy, four-year lump. My goodness! That would overwhelm the stoutest heart. And it doesn't have to be like that. We're going to do it the easy way. First, we deal with one semester. Then the next one. Then the one after that. What we do is stay in the NOW and think of it all as a beautiful string of colored beads slowly slipping through our fingers, one at a time."

"Great," Steve said. "Just so you remember the first bead drops in exactly six months."

"Six months," Mom sighed happily, "Imagine. Six long, lovely months to get together that teeny, tiny sum of money."

FIVE

For a while after Mom got into her meditating and chanting, things seemed to settle down. Like Mary said, "Sure, it's weird. But nobody knows about it but us and she must be handling her slime-bag boss better. She's been home on time every night for over a month now and he's not calling here nights, throwing his filthy tantrums."

It came to an end one Saturday when she was meditating - in the lotus position, of course - in the living room. I was curious about what she was going to be affirming that day so I stayed put in the kitchen dawdling over the old cornflakes, eavesdropping.

"Om-m-m-m," she goes. "I see abundance flowing towards me like a mighty river." I hear a deep, indrawn breath and I know she's getting ready for the next Om-m-m... only right then there's this horrific crashing sound coming from the garage.

I stuck my head in the living room wondering if it's gotten through Mom's trance and I see her eyes briefly startle open but she isn't moving. Instead she's taking another deep breath and chanting, "Peace lies within." Then Mary's standing in front of her looking seriously upset. Like, ballistic.

"That wonder kid of yours just took out the garage door," she screams.

I see Mom's teeth clench but she isn't opening her eyes. "I can't concern myself with externals just now, Mary," she says with deliberate calm. "Baseballs and other flying objects have been crashing into that door since we moved here." She puts the fingers of both hands to her solar plexus, inhales deeply and chants, "The inner life is the true life."

"You're not going to be too concerned with your inner life," Mary shrieks, "when you take a look at the outer life of your old shit-mobile and the garage door."

That gets her eyes open. "My car?" she yelps, scrambling to her feet and following Mary outside.

'Course I go too and there's Steve, looking dazed, staring at the car imbedded in the garage door.

"This heap of yours nearly killed me," he yells seeing Mom behind Mary. "I put the damn thing in park, got out to open the garage door and next thing I know it's coming right at me. It must've slipped out of gear. It could have run me down. Broken my legs..."

"Oh, God," Mom's moaning, looking Steve over. "Are you sure you're OK? How about the car? Will it still run?"

"Yes, to both," he says. "But the garage door won't. Look at the runners. Trashed. You'll have to replace the whole thing."

Right away we've got the old Mom back. "Oh, God," she's moaning. "It'll cost hundreds. Maybe thousands. How'm I supposed to come up with that kind of money with college just a few months away?"

I followed her back into the house just in time to see her kick the inner peace book across the room and hear her yelling, "One thing you forgot to mention, Oh, Great Maharishi! How does inner peace pay bills?"

Right away I could tell we wouldn't be hearing any more om-ing for a while.

It wasn't the end of the How-To books though. We heard about them all from, *How To Pinch Pennies at the Supermarket*, to *How to Grow a Fortune*, to *How to Make Yourself Over in Thirty Days*.

And then came a bunch that outlasted all the others and got us from where we were to where we are today.

"Have any of you ever noticed," Mom began, looking up from one of those books, "how if you really want something, you get it?"

As I recall, nobody answered but she went on anyway.

"This book's making me realize that every single thing I ever really wanted – I mean, wanted to the point of obsession – I got. And what is obsession but thoughts, ideas, repeating themselves over and over in your head to the exclusion of everything else? In other words, you get what you think about. Thoughts have power. They act like magnets. They attract. Think negative thoughts and you attract negative results. Think positive thoughts and you attract positive results. Thoughts create your life. They create the reality you live.

"I'm also realizing something else," she goes on even though all she's gotten from us is yawns. "And it's that the things I wanted and didn't get were things I didn't really believe were possible." She made a face. "Like me making a fortune in real estate."

"So what did you ever get? From your thoughts, I mean." I asked.

"Well, when I was about, oh... eleven or twelve I suppose I was, I wanted a horse of my own so badly I couldn't think straight. My head was filled with horses. I spent every cent I could get my hands on for riding lessons, read every book on horses I could find, collected little china horses. Why, I'd even ride my bike for miles just to get a look at a horse grazing in a field and I'd..."

"We get the picture, Mom." Mary said testily. "You liked horses."

"Go on, Mom, tell us the rest," Steve said, throwing a cushion at Mary.

"Well, you can imagine I nearly drove my parents crazy pestering for a horse of my own. 'No,' they said. 'Horses cost money. Saddles and bridles cost money. So does hay and corn and shoes and places to keep them.' Their list of no's was as long as my list of pleases."

"So what happened?" I coaxed when her voice trailed off and she got a faraway look in her eyes, remembering, I guess, how it had been for her when she was a kid, goofy over horses.

"I got a horse of my own," she said triumphantly, snapping back into focus and beaming around at us.

"You did?"

"No way!"

"How come you never told us about it before?"

"I thought I had. Well, you knew I had a horse. I guess I just never told you how I got it."

"You just told us." Mary snapped. "You thought about it, obsessed over it, and one morning, I bet you woke up and there it was, tied to the end of your bed."

"One of these days..." Steve warned her.

"It was one of the horses I rode my bike to see." Mom went on. "I was leaning over the gate, just watching it graze, thinking how beautiful it was, you know, and a lady came by in a car and saw me and stopped. Turned out it was her children's horse, or used to be. Only they'd grown up and gone away and she said I could buy it if I would give it a good home. I said I'd love to only I couldn't because I didn't have any money or a place to give it a home."

"Poor you, huh? What did the lady say?"

"She said it could stay right where it was. She owned that field and all the other fields around. And then she asked if I got an allowance. I told her, yes, a dollar a week."

"A dollar a week," the lady said thoughtfully. "That makes fifty-two dollars a year. Tell you what, if you bring me thirty dollars a year for the next four years, the horse, along with its saddle and bridle, is yours."

We were all hanging on every word Mom was saying by then, even Mary, all of us forgetting our favorite TV show was coming on any minute.

"You must have been blown away. What'd you tell her?" one of us asked.

"I told her I'd go straight home and ask my parents and could I have her phone number so we could call."

"And..?"

"I got the horse! And that's what I'm trying to tell you now. I wanted something to the point of obsession. I thought about it, imagined it day and night, saw myself as having it, and I got it. Do you realize how amazing that is? How magical? Thoughts have power! They attract! But... and this is a big but, you have to believe that what you want is possible. If you have doubts, it doesn't work. You know why? Because you literally get what you think about. That means, if you have doubts, as I did in real estate, you'll get the doubts instead because doubt and worry are thoughts too! I tell you, you really do get what you think about!"

She jumped up from her chair looking really excited and began walking around the room, touching stuff, straightening stuff, but not really seeing any of it.

"Do any of you understand what I'm saying?" she asked, stopping her pacing to look at us, wondering, I guess, how come she was so excited and we weren't. I mean, I could tell from their faces that Steve and Mary were as clueless as I was.

"Come on," she urged. "Think about it. This is exciting. It's amazing. It means we have control over our lives. It means everybody can have, or be, anything they want. All they have to do is think about it, see themselves behaving as if they already have it... are it... and it happens."

"Sounds like loony tunes to me," Mary said. "Just like the om-ing."

"I got my ten-speed bike when I was fourteen," Steve said, rolling from his back to his stomach on the floor and propping his chin in his hands. "I worked my butt of mowing lawns to pay for it though. I don't see what's the big deal. Seems to me if you want something that bad and your parent's can't, or won't, give it to you, then you go out and earn the money. Yeah, OK. I got what I wanted same as you. So what?"

"But don't you see?" Mom said, trying not to sound too exasperated. "You had to want it first. That means you thought about it. You became obsessed with it. Ask me, I remember! That's all you talked about. And don't tell me you weren't imagining yourself riding around on it. Showing it off to your friends. Maybe winning races with it. You thought about it, imagined it detail by detail, expected it, and you got it."

"I got it because I paid for it." Steve said flatly, yawning and closing his eyes.

"OK, OK," Mom said. "Let's leave things that cost money out of it. Let's talk about... Let's see... Events. How many times have you wanted to go someplace real bad. A party. The beach. A rock concert? Disneyworld? Or what about excelling in a sport? It's all you can think about. You imagine yourself being there... winning the event. And next thing you know, you're at the show... On the team..."

"I'm always imagining myself dancing like John Travolta," I said. "But it's never happened."

"It would if you believed it possible and thought about it twenty-four hours a day. You'd study his videos. Practice. You *would* dance like John Travolta. The reason you don't is because you don't *believe* it's possible."

"Get real, Mom," Mary snorted. "That clod dancing like John Travolta!"

"I didn't say he could be John Travolta, Mary," Mom snapped. "I said he could dance like John Travolta. Anyway, do you understand now how thought and imagination make things happen?"

"Sort of," Steve said. But you could tell he was just saying it because if he didn't Mom would try even harder to explain it and he wasn't up for it.

"I'm too tired to think right now," Mary said, faking a yawn.

I didn't say anything. I found out a long time ago that being the youngest lets me off the hook a lot.

"We'll talk about it some more when we're all a bit fresher," Mom said. "I'll try and explain it better."

"You did just fine, Mom," Mary said quickly. "I'll let you know next time I want something real bad and after I've earned enough to go out and buy it, you'll get to say, 'I told you so'."

"Oh, Mary," Mom sighed. "How'd you ever get to be so cynical?"

"That's not being cynical," Mary said. "That's being realistic. Good old fashioned supply and demand. And if all this were true, how come you didn't keep on with the imagining? I mean, this family could sure use a lot of neat stuff right now, including money."

"Because... I didn't realize what I'd done. Didn't make the connection. I just thought I got lucky. So did everyone else. You should have heard them. 'You're such a lucky little girl!' was all anyone could say. As for money now... Well, I... Well, money has never been that important to me..." she broke off, looking sheepish, because we were all laughing at her.

"The way you scrimp and save and worry about it all the time, I'd say money was very important to you," Steve said.

"Only because there's never enough to go around. But that was before I realized what I've just been telling you. From now on though, you can bet I'm going to be imagining a whole new way of life and..."

"Yeah, yeah," Mary said impatiently. "Honest to God, Mom, just get us some money, OK? We all need new clothes, especially me. All this homemade stuff is ruining my image. And we need a decent car. The house is falling down. Needs paint..."

"I will," Mom said. "But first I'm going to start with something little."

"Why? Why think little when you can think big?" Mary asked. "It's free either way."

"Because... I need to think it all out some more. I'm going to need practice. My adult mind has to revert, in many ways, to a child's mind. I mean, kids believe in magic, that's how come I got a horse. I didn't *believe* in the obstacles my parents saw. Right now, I'm going to think about getting Steve through college because," she looked at him sideways, "we don't have any money."

"We've got the first semester, haven't we?" he asked, coming upright in a big hurry.

"Not quite. But don't worry. We both want you to go, so you'll go. Thought creates reality."

As best I can remember, we dropped the subject after that. I guess we all saw it as just another one of Mom's wacky notions. That, or we took it for just plain old day dreaming. The kind of talk most families have, I guess, of when they're all grown up or world famous or whatever it is they're looking forward to. It was only long afterwards that we remembered that day and, piecing the conversation together again, realized that was when the wheels started turning. They turned slow and there were a lot of times they didn't turn at all, but that was the beginning.

Anyway, nothing spectacular happened right afterwards to make us remember. I mean, Mom didn't dream up another horse or get us new clothes or a new car or fix up the house. In fact, nothing changed at all so what was there to think about?

Six

One thing I do remember about those days though was the way time seemed to speed up for me. I mean, maybe it was because I was getting older and busier but it seemed like one minute we're sitting around talking our way through those long winter evenings, the next, the big heat's back, Steve's graduated, school's out, and Steve and I are back at our lawn jobs and dock repairs. Only that summer we worked like there wasn't going to be another because Steve wanted all the money he could get his hands on for college.

Some days we'd have up to six lawns to get through. The first couple I could take but, man, by the time we'd pull up on our bikes, towing the mowers, to the fourth, fifth and sixth, that grass would look so high and those yards so big, I'd wonder what I was doing there. I mean, who was going to college anyway?

"A swim would sure feel good right now, wouldn't it?" I'd hint. "Let's come back and do this one tomorrow."

"Can't," he'd say, busy unhitching his mower and attaching the catcher bag. "We've already got four lined up for tomorrow. Besides, we said we'd do it today."

"Yeah, but..."

"No buts. We're doing it today. Move your ass."

"Move your own damn ass."

"What's it look like I'm doing? Setting up for a snooze? And you ought to be grateful. You're making the same money as me and you can spend it any way you want. Besides, think of the goodwill I'm building up for you next year. I've got these neighborhoods all sewn up."

Next year. I hated the way "next year" and "next fall" and, "When I'm gone don't forget to do this or that," was slipping into every conversation. And it wasn't just Steve saying it. It was Mom and Mary, too.

"Go with Steve and watch how he changes the oil in my car," or, "...fixes the washing machine," or, "...cuts back the palm trees," Mom would say. "In September that'll be your job."

And Mary, who'd fought with Steve all her life, suddenly couldn't do enough for him. She had a full time, baby-sitting job herself that summer and was hardly ever home, but at breakfast, and again at dinner, she and Mom would practically knock each other over in the kitchen, fussing over him and waiting on him and just plain sitting and staring at him.

If it sounds like I was jealous, I was. Not of the attention they were giving him but of his time. Time I figured was mine. I guess the fact was, none of us wanted him to go away. Couldn't imagine our lives without him.

"I know," Mary said one time, "Let's all move up to Gainesville. Sell this place and buy one up there. Then Steve can go to school and still live at home."

"Give me a break," Steve groaned.

"Easier said than done, Mary," Mom said. "Besides, it'll be good for Steve to be out on his own. That's part of what college is all about, learning to handle life without your family there full of unwanted advice. It'll be good for us, too. We'll learn that we can get along just fine without him although..." she sort of gulped, "I can't imagine how."

So one hot, muggy dawn at the end of August, the sun just coming up, mean and blood-red like someone threw open the doors to a furnace, we headed for Gainesville. I wondered if Mom was as worried as I was about whether her old heap was going to make it there and back. Just about everything Steve owned was jammed in it as well as us and a half dozen cookie tins with sharp corners that Mary had filled with homemade cookies and tears. Tied to the back, in the best way we could figure to tie it, was Steve's old bike.

"I can't take these family outings." Mary shuddered, shoving a cookie tin into my ribs with her elbow, "They're all sentiment and no class. Ugh!"

"It's you takes the class out of them," I told her, shoving the cookies back her way.

"I'm glad I don't know anyone up there," Steve said. "This car and that bike on the back are embarrassing enough without you two. I wish you'd both stayed home in your playpens where you belong."

"Maybe now's a perfect time for me to explain my theory about thought?" Mom suggested brightly.

"No!" we all howled in unison.

"If I don't get to theorize, you two don't get to talk to one another, OK?" Mom said. And then a few hours later when we swung off the Interstate and were stuck in a traffic jam in the middle of Gainesville, she broke the silence herself, saying, "It's like another planet! I never saw so many kids and bicycles in my life. Aren't there any adults around?"

I could see what she meant. Go into downtown, our town, on a weekend, or even a weekday for that matter, and if you're lucky you might get to see ten people out on the sidewalks. If you're real lucky, one or two of them might be under sixty years old.

In Gainesville, the sidewalks and stores and streets were packed with kids, some jammed six to eight to a car, a bunch whipping around on roller-blades and skate boards, a mob hanging around some dude with a shaved head making a speech from the top of a trash can outside McDonalds. Man, it was wild. Like the whole town was having a party.

"Will you look at the girls?" Steve said, nearly wrecking looking at two of them dodging between cars in cut-offs that were really cut off.

"How about the guys?" Mary yelped, twisting in her seat every which way, burying me under suitcases and cookies.

"Wow-wee! Did you ever see so many cute ones? All in one place! Maybe I'll go to college after all."

"Won't do you any good," I told her. "These are college kids. Way too smart to look at you."

"Shithead!" she hissed at me.

"I heard that, Mary," Mom said, "and it's lucky for you I have other things to deal with today."

There was a lot to deal with. It took us nearly all day, standing in lines, to get Steve signed up for, and into, everything and everyplace he needed to be.

"I've never spent so much money in one day in my life," Mom sighed, pulling her check book out over and over again. "When's it all going to end?"

"In about four years, I'd say." Mary said. "But don't worry. I've changed my mind again. Guys or no guys, I'm not going to college. I couldn't put up with all this crap."

"You wear me out, Mary," Mom said. "We'll get Steve settled in today. Tomorrow, we'll turn our attention to you."

"No, we won't," Mary said. "I've decided. Just now. I'm not going to college. Not ever. No matter what."

"We'll talk about it later," Mom said firmly. "Let's go find your room - dorm - whatever it's called, Steve."

"It's my life..." Mary began, her hands going up to her hips, ready for a fight, but we weren't interested and left her there, talking to herself.

We found the dorm at the top of four flights of stairs. Somebody who thought they were an artist had painted larger than life pictures of athletes in psychedelic colors at the top of each flight of stairs which broke the climb up some but didn't do much for art.

Whatever the room, dorm, was, it wasn't worth the climb.

"Oh, dear..." Mom said on a deep sigh.

"Sooner you than me, dude," I said to Steve.

"They couldn't pay me to stay in that dump," Mary said, catching up with us, then backing out quicker than I'd seen her move in a long time.

Steve didn't say anything. Just sort of gulped a couple of times.

It was a dump. About the size of a closet with bare, dirty walls, dirty floors, two cruddy iron beds with nasty, stained, inch-thick mattresses, two old dressers, their drawers stuck permanently half in, half out, their knobs missing. A broken Venetian blind hung at the window like it was trying to decide whether to stay where it was or give up and let go. When we carried Steve's trunk in and plunked it down, it decided and let go with a crash. "Takes the worry out of it," I said, but nobody laughed.

"Well, honey," Mom said, trying to sound cheerful, "Maybe it won't look so bad when we get your bed made up. You could put some posters up. I'll send you a piece of carpet for the floor. Maybe a plant would be nice..." Her smile faded. "Lord, it really is awful, isn't it? Imagine that we have to pay for you to stay in it."

"It's OK," Steve said. "I'll fix it up. You won't know it next time you see it. Why don't you guys leave now?"

"Ho-ney!" Mom protested. "We've got to get you settled. It's so dirty. Maybe we can borrow a mop from somewhere. At least we could clean up the floor a little. Maybe fix that blind."

"I told you it's fine. Why don't you just head on home now? You've got a long drive ahead of you. You've got work in the morning. The kids have school."

"Watch who you're calling a kid," Mary warned.

"Let's go home, Mom," I said, guessing Steve was really depressed and needed us out of there to deal with it.

Mom knew it, too, but she had a hard time dragging herself away.

"OK," she said at last. "You're right. We should be on our way. Walk us out to the car. I can't even remember where we parked. Feels like we've been here for weeks."

We found the car, looking shabbier than ever and strangely forlorn stripped of all Steve's gear. We piled in and made feeble jokes about our college man and then Steve was walking away from us across the worn-out grass between the buildings, looking so alone in the midst of all the groups of lounging, laughing students that I wondered if he had a lump in his throat as big as the one in mine.

It was weird driving home with Mary at the wheel instead of Steve.

"I'm the eldest around here now," she told me, grinning into the rear-view mirror where she could see my reflection, "and don't you forget it."

I knew she'd never let me so I didn't bother answering.

SEVEN

"Life without Steve," as Mom called it, wasn't near as bad as we'd let ourselves think it would be. It was as if we'd done all our missing him while he was still there - the way we'd hung all over him - so when he was really gone it was more of a relief than anything else because we didn't have to dread it anymore.

Still, the first couple weeks after he left I'd forget and go running into his room to get him to help me with a flat tire or homework and, "What'd that sucker have to go off to college for?" I'd ask myself, standing in the doorway looking at the strangely neat, shades-drawn look of it.

Weird how many things I'd always had him do for me, just because he was there, I guess, that all along I must've known how to do myself, because I did them. Unless it was something really new to me and then I'd wait for Mom to get home. She'd forget too. "Go ask Steve," she'd say, "he'll know." And then her face would go blank and she'd say, "What'd he have to grow up for? We need him." And turning to me she'd add, "Do me a favor and take your time growing up, OK?"

It wasn't worth asking Mary anything. She's made a career of not knowing useful things that might make her think and besides, she was in her senior year then and busy with the million guys that were chasing her although what they saw in her, don't ask me.

"What about homework, Mary?" Mom would call, catching her as she flew in and out of the house juggling school and dates and football games and baby-sitting like she had to live her whole demented life in one day.

"It's fine, Mom," Mary would call back. "All done."

"You've got your SATs Saturday, remember?"

"I remember, Mom. And do you remember I'm not going to college?" And she'd be out the door and into the car of whichever dude she was dating at the time.

"Where did I go wrong with her?" Mom would ask when the squeals and roars of burning rubber and thudding music were far enough away that we could talk without yelling.

"Nowhere," I'd tell her. "Mary is Mary, is all." Once I added, "Two out of three ain't bad," but she didn't buy that at all.

"A parent," she said sternly, "goes for three out of three."

"Well," I said, and you can guess how much I hated saying it knowing what a first class pain I thought Mary was in those days, "you've got three out of three. Compared to all the air-head girls I know in school, she's really not that bad. Just because she doesn't want to go to college, doesn't mean you went wrong."

"But she should go," Mom insisted. "Nowadays more than ever, girls need careers. I don't ever want her to find herself in the position I'm in if a man walks out on her."

"You've got to be kidding!" I said. "Mary acting like you? She's the one who almost single-handedly brought you into the twentieth century, remember? Nobody'll ever walk out on her because she'd walk first. Besides, she's never studied here. Never done homework her whole life. What makes you think she'd study up there?"

Mom shrugged. "It would be good for her. A stepping stone to adult life. And fun. College can be a lot of fun."

"She's having plenty of fun here. At least, her idea of fun. And it's not costing you a dime. Did you ever think about that?"

Of course, Mary didn't go to college. Nobody but Mom ever thought she would.

What Mary did was take matters into her own hands right after her high school graduation ceremony.

"I'm so proud of you honey," Mom blubbered, out in the parking lot, "And so sorry I have to rush back to that darned old office. But I'll hurry home tonight and we'll celebrate before you go to your parties. And we'll have a nice long chat about your future and college. You will see Jeff gets home, won't you?"

The dust hadn't settled on Mom's departing car than Mary's whipping off her cap and gown, throwing them in the back seat of the dude-of-the-week's car, and telling him, "Be a baby-doll and take me and the kid over to J.C., OK?"

"You're supposed to be getting me home, remember?" I said.

"Chill," Mary said. "First chance we get, you're home."

"What're we going to J.C. for?" I wanted to know. "I told the guys I'd take them out in the canoe. They're waiting on me."

"Let 'em wait," Mary said. "We're going to J.C. so I can enroll in a travel agent course. There's a whole big world out there and I'm gonna see all of it."

"Does Mom know?"

"No. And don't go blabbing to her before I do. That's why we're going now. Today. Before she can get going on her, 'You have to go to college,' routine one more time."

"She'll know when the bills come pouring in."

In answer Mary waved a wad of money. "No, she won't. All those creep-o brats I baby-sat the last two years? They're paying."

By the time Mom got over all that, Mary had a job, a "career" she called it, a brand-new car she got Dad to co-sign for, and was getting ready for her first "FAM" trip - FAM being short for familiarization - meaning you get to go see for yourself the places you're going to be sending your clients.

"You're a miracle worker, Mary. How'd you do all this?" Mom asked on the way to the restaurant Mary was taking us to to celebrate her first paycheck.

"Well," Mary said, fluttering her eyelashes and lisping like she was three years old, "I wanted it real, real bad and I thought about it real, real hard, just like you told me, and one morning I woke up and ta-da! I had it all!"

"Oh," Mom said. And then, brightening, "Of course! That's the only way you could have done it. You thought about it, imagined it, and then you became it. You're living your dream. I'm glad you've been listening to me. I didn't think you heard a word I said."

"I heard you, Momma," Mary said. "I always hear you. I just don't always agree with you. I don't now. I was just kidding before. I didn't get this job sitting around imagining it. I got it because I went out and studied for it and applied for it and earned it. There's no other way."

"But you had to think about it first. You saw yourself doing it, imagined all the travel, and then you took the necessary action." Mom insisted. "If you hadn't you'd be doing something else. Going to college or working at McDonald's."

"I did. Of course, I did. But then I went out and did what I had to do. Nobody came knocking on my door."

"Ma-ry! If you'd just stop and think a minute, you'd see we're both saying the same thing. In fact, you're living what I only seem to theorize. You zeroed in on what you wanted. You imagined it! Didn't let doubt or obstacles cloud your mind. And you got what you thought about. Your actions mirrored your thoughts."

"Yes? Then why don't you practice what you preach? Walk the talk? You're a little short on action, aren't you? How come you're still working at a job you hate. How come you don't get busy and imagine a job you'd love and take the necessary action?"

"Good question. Well... The fact is I don't want any kind of job at all. Jobs to me are not satisfying, challenging, or exciting. At heart I'm very domesticated. I like making things, creating things... Being at home messing around with my own little projects."

"Then why haven't you imagined a life for yourself where you can stay home and mess around? What's stopping you?"

"Nothing's stopping me. Only... Well, there are days, months even, when, I'm ashamed to say, I get so caught up in the frenzy of day-to-day living, I just plain forget to think about what I'd really like to be doing. I forget to dream beyond the day."

"And what is it you really want?"

"I just told you. I want a life without bosses and ringing phones and deadlines. It all frazzles me so I forget who I am and what I want. I want to be free. That's it. I want the freedom to learn to be really me. And, of course, the money to pay for that freedom."

"Yea for the money!"

"Yes, money! Enough of it for all of us so that we don't have to waste so much of our lives figuring ways to stretch it. And so Jeff won't have to work his way through college the way Steve is. And I want a husband. It seems to me you have to go through one marriage to learn how to be married and I'm..."

"A husband?" I interrupted. "You mean you want another one?"

"Of course she does, dork," Mary broke in. "We're all growing up. Even you in your own idiot way. You don't think she's going to spend the rest of her life watching the crab grass grow while she waits for us to come home for a visit, do you?"

"How would I know?" I said. "I never thought about it." But it did seem to me Mom was going to need something more along the lines of an act of God than imagination if she was going to have all the things she'd just talked about.

Mary must've thought so, too, because she was quiet for a least a minute, which is like a normal person being quiet for an hour, before she said, "Wow. You don't want much, do you? It's one thing to think you can 'imagine' things into your life, Mom, but don't expect me to believe that's how you plan to get a husband. Husbands you go out and meet or get introduced to. They don't pop out of people's heads."

"Yes they do if by 'head' you mean imagination. Thoughts attract people the same way they attract situations and things. I don't see why you have such a hard time understanding that. I keep telling you that the mind works like a magnet. It automatically draws to you whatever it is you hold in your thoughts, good and bad. That's why you have to be so careful about what thoughts you allow in your mind because whatever they are, you'll live the results. Exactly so. Remember when I first went out to work and imagined the very worst all the time and remember what happened?"

"You got the worst. The pits."

"Yes, I did and serve me right. I brought it all on myself. Whereas you, Mary, you went out fearlessly. You expected to achieve. To succeed. And look at you now!"

"All right, Mother," Mary snapped. "We know how it goes. You tell us enough. What you don't do is show us. You came up with this wild idea way long ago. Before Steve went away, even. One big burst of talk and then... nothing."

"That's not fair, Mary, I've done lots of little things." Mom gasped, all indignant.

We were in the restaurant by then, the same one we always go to when there's something in the family to celebrate. It's dark in there until your eyes get used to it and then you see that there are a lot of little rooms strung in a row, each one a clutter of red-clothed tables with candles. Wonderful smells of fresh baked bread and garlic sauces hang over everything making you think you're starved even when you've just eaten a peanut butter sandwich.

The place is always packed and when Mom came out with her, "I've done lots of little things," we were standing in the lobby with a few other people waiting, like the sign said, for the hostess to seat us. "Enough to know..." she continued loudly in that embarrassing way adults have of talking in front of a room full of strangers like they really want to know our business.

"Tell us at the table," Mary said quickly.

"You two are always so uptight," Mom complained in the same loud voice and I could have killed her but she didn't say anymore about her ideas until we were having desert and probably wouldn't have then except I reminded her. I mean, Mary can scoff and sneer all she wants about this 'getting what you think about' stuff, but I kind of like the sound of it myself. Especially the way Mom tells it. It seems exciting and magical to me that everything you could ever want comes out of your own imagination.

I wished I hadn't pushed for details that particular time though because the stuff she came up with sounded pitiful even to me and put some serious doubts in my mind. And, of course, Mary laughed and yawned it all right out of the water.

Like, for instance, she tried telling us that getting the outside of the house painted was the result of her imagining. As though, for Pete's sake, we woke up one morning and found the whole place painted when, in fact, it took us three weekends of grief to paint it ourselves.

"How can you say that?" Mary snorted with such indignation that the candle flame before us leveled out sideways and died in the liquid wax at its base. "That was me out there on a ladder painting. Not your imagination. Or the tooth fairy."

"Yes, of course it was," Mom said. "I was out there too, remember? The point I'm making is that you get what you think about. And I thought about the house looking the way it's supposed to look and not like skid row. If I'd thought about all the bills coming in and Steve's next semester and how I'm not managing to save a single penny no matter how hard I economize, then you can bet the house would never have been painted. But I got what I thought about."

Mary yawned. "Let's go home now," she said.

"I wish I knew how to get through to you," Mom said, frowning. "How about the fact that Steve is finishing up his sophomore year in college? Does that convince either of you of anything?"

"Like what? He's working practically full time. Your busting your a... Just forget it."

"Truly, there's none so blind as those who will not see," Mom said wearily. "From now on I'll just have to show you instead of telling you. On a day-to-day basis."

"Oh, my God," Mary groaned. "It's bad enough once a year. I don't think I could take it day to day."

What Mom did, after that, was tell us what she was working on, "visualizing" as she put it, so we could see for ourselves. It was all pretty dumb stuff to me, stuff I wouldn't have made a project over. And always the kind of stuff you wondered wouldn't have come her way anyway. Like a book she wanted real bad that was out of print. She went everywhere looking for it. Book stores. Libraries. Garage sales. And every book shelf in every friend's house she ever went into.

"Don't worry," she told Mary and me, looking at us like she actually thought we were. "I'll find it. In my imagination I already have it, I see myself reading it."

"Gag me with a spoon," Mary muttered and I only wished I could.

A stranger knocked on our front door one Saturday morning not too long after the search began, the book Mom was looking for in her hand, and asked would we please give it to our next door neighbor? They weren't home just then, she explained, and she had borrowed it over a year ago and only just come across it and couldn't believe she still had it. She was so embarrassed she'd run right over to return it.

"Coincidence," Mary said flatly when Mom got done jumping up and down saying, "I told you so!"

Coincidence was a word you don't use around Mom anymore and Mary knew it.

"How many, many times am I going to have to tell you that there IS NO SUCH THING AS COINCIDENCE?" she demanded of Mary, sitting down on a bar stool facing her, the precious book clutched in both hands.

"No more times," I interrupted in what I hoped was a stern manner because I'd heard it a million times since she'd come to that conclusion a while back and I didn't want to have to listen to it again either.

When Mom has an idea coming you can practically hear it rumbling around in the back of her head and you learn to brace yourself for it because, like I said, once she gets one you're going to be hearing about it for a long, long time. She's like a dog worrying a bone with it, kicking it around in her mind, and ours, for things to back it up. Finally she gets it worked out to where she can put it into words and then she's like a kid with a new toy, bringing it out, making sure we get the point, every chance she gets.

Of course, if you go along with her ideas of getting what you think about, then it's obvious that there's no such thing as coincidence. I figured that out for myself. I mean, how could there be if, really, you are thinking your life into happening all the time and imagining you've already got all the things you want or need?

Like the way we got new carpeting. "I always said one of the first thing I'd do in this house when I got my hands on some extra money was to rip out that nasty old shag carpeting, didn't I?" Mom said the day our awesome new carpeting was installed and we were sitting around admiring it.

"You didn't get your hands on any money though, did you?" Mary said sweetly, sliding out of her chair and onto the carpet so she could run her fingers through the thick pile.

"That proves my point even more," Mom said. "I was focused on the end result, not the ways and means of getting it. Besides," she added with just a touch of sarcasm, "I imagined the room carpeted in carpet, not money. If I'd received money I'd have spent it on something else, paid a few bills, even though the carpet was important to me. So important, in fact, that it materialized before our very eyes."

"Give me patience, God," Mary groaned, closing her eyes and clenching her fists. "You just got lucky those rich SOB's ordered the wrong color, is all," she added when she could bring herself to speak again.

Mom was working for an interior decorator at that time, Harry's Harmonious Homes - Heartburn Harry, Mary called him - and had arranged for the installation of carpeting for some out-of-town people. When the "clients" came to town to look over their beach-front condo all hell broke loose because the wrong carpeting had gone down. Of course, there was a lot of screaming and crying and threatened law suits but when it all died down a letter was found in the files, in the client's own handwriting, showing they had specifically ordered exactly what was on the floor.

Considering the fuss they'd made they couldn't hardly back down and say they were wrong, so they had it all ripped out and we got to save the 'wrong' stuff from being hauled off to the dump.

"If I just got lucky," Mom persisted, "then tell me how come it's exactly, but exactly, the color I always wanted in here?"

"Beats me," Mary said. "We're not allowed to have coincidences around here anymore, are we? I guess you must have forged that letter."

But Mom wasn't listening. In her mind, the day she'd thought of new carpeting in a particular color was the day the whole chain of events was set in motion. As simple and clear as ABC from her point of view, as clouded and far out as a foggy day from Mary's. Besides, she was getting that faraway look in her eyes that I knew so well, and when she blinked back into focus, she said, "I've been thinking and you know what?"

"Don't ask," Mary yelped at me, jumping to her feet and heading for her room.

"What?" I asked.

"I do believe that the future creates the present, not the past, as we've always believed. And that means we're not at the mercy of the past. Another thing I've always believed."

"Come again," I said, yelling to be heard over the sound of Mary's screamed, "Oh, my God!' and the crash of her door slamming.

"Think about it. If you get what you think about, the thoughts come first. Imagination projects them into the future. Then you grow towards them and they become the present and finally the past. It's easy to understand if you think of inventions. Someone starts out with an idea of what they want to achieve. That puts it into the future while they work towards it. The accomplishment brings it into the present, and then it goes into the history books. That definitely means we're not at the mercy of the past."

"Mom," I said. "I'm not up for any more ideas tonight, OK? I'm going to bed."

"OK, sweetie, sleep well," she said absent-mindedly, too busy with her pasts and presents and futures to pay me much attention.

Like I said earlier, her ideas came non-stop and I liked listening to most of them but no matter how hard I tried, I could never really believe her one hundred per cent, and I couldn't disbelieve her one hundred per cent either. So that's how I left it. I mean, if thinking her thoughts kept her happy, why not?

And then some turkey up in Gainesville ripped off Steve's bike. Such a little nothing event it seemed to me then, but by the time Steve graduated a year later and our lives changed forever, not one of us kids, not even Mary who right up to the very end, thought Mom was a space walker, would ever again tune her out when she got that faraway look in her eyes and said, "I've been thinking and you know what?"

Eight

When Steve's letter came telling us his bike had been stolen you'd have thought someone had torn off his arms and legs and thrown what was left of him in a Dempsey-Dumpster the way Mom carried on.

"You're over-reacting, Mom." Mary said through clenched teeth.

"That's for sure," I said, agreeing with Mary for once. "Sure it was a neat bike back when he bought it, but don't forget that was a long, long time ago. It was already looking kind of junky when he took it up to school and that was three years ago. Three years of being chained up in the rain and the heat and the cold. I saw it last time we were up there. You probably did, too, only you didn't recognize it. It was a wreck. A pile of rust. Whoever stole it must've been drunk or stupid. Both, probably."

"That's not the point at all, Jeff," Mom said, almost in tears. "The point is that he still needs it, has had to use it, all these years. Your brother is twenty-one years old now. He's a man, not a boy. And a man shouldn't have to be concerned about some jerk stealing a pile of rust that belonged in the dump a long time ago. He should have a car."

She sat down slowly, massaging her forehead with her finger tips. "It's all my fault. Don't you see, by always thinking economy, scrimping and scraping, worrying about the next dollar, I've made him – us – poor."

"Oh, brother," Mary sighed. "Where's my violin?"

"Never mind the sarcasm, Mary. What I'm saying is true. My thoughts have created this situation we're in. By always seeing myself as this hard-working, self-sacrificing, single-Mom who, no matter how hard she tries, never seems to get ahead, I've put us exactly where we are today." She groaned. "I've brought you up all wrong. Taught you to make do... To compromise."

"Not me, you didn't," Mary snorted. "I never bought any of it."

"All we've done all these years is shortchange ourselves," Mom rattled on, "Or at least, I have. As though it's an honor to do without. It's not. It's settling for less. Copping out. As though I somehow think we don't deserve better. And I'm sick to death of people telling me that Steve will appreciate his education the more because he earned ninety-five percent of it himself. I... It's all bullshit!"

"Mo-ther!" Mary gasped, genuinely shocked. "Your language!"

"Well, it's true," Mom went on. "He'd appreciate his college years and look back on them with a lot more pleasure if he'd had a little fun along the way instead of working every single minute he's not in class. Plus having to find jobs down here every vacation he gets. He needs a break."

"You said it all at the beginning, Mom." Mary said. "Steve's a man now. He can deal with it. Chill."

But Mom wasn't about to chill. "How many kids do you know," she asked, turning to me, "right here in this neighborhood, who didn't have a car when they were sixteen? Or eighteen at the very latest?"

"None," I said. "Only Mary and she got her own."

"Oh, Mary..." Mom faltered. "Everything I'm saying goes for you, too. I'm so sorry. And what's Steve supposed to do when he graduates?" she asked, turning back to me indignantly, as though it was all my fault. "Thumb rides? How's he supposed to go out on interviews? Borrow your bike? Dressed in a suit and tie? No!"

"He'll be all right, Mom," Mary said. "He can borrow my car till he gets going... buys one of his own."

"That's sweet, Mary. But it's not the answer. I have to do better!" Mom said, slamming her fist down on the counter.

"Watch her, Jeff," Mary said, only half joking. "She's really cooking."

"Yes, I am," Mom said. "I don't know where I've been these last few years not thinking this through. Not realizing where my thoughts were taking us. I've been burying my head in the sand, I guess. Not willing to take on the responsibility of myself. Still... It's not too late is it? We can get him a car. At least by the time he graduates, we can. Why not? Don't you think he hasn't wanted one all these years? Of course he has. How must he feel up there, a senior and no car? Oh, it's so awful. I'm so ashamed. How can he ask girls - all those beautiful girls - on dates? How could I have been so thick?"

"Maybe because he never asked for one?" Mary suggested.

"Of course he never asked for one," Mom said irritably. "How could he? How could you, when you both know perfectly well I'm flat broke?"

"If you can't afford one, how are we going to get him one now?" I wondered out loud.

"How should I know?" she exploded. "But I will. A new one. All paid for. Free and clear. How's that?"

"Brave words, Mom," Mary said. "Brave words. But that's all it ever is with you. Just a lot of words. Never any action. How're you..."

"I just said, I don't know. But if I can imagine us giving him one, and I can certainly do that, then it will happen. My thoughts will make it happen. What kind of car does he want? Do either of you know?"

"A BMW," I said.

"Bright red," Mary said.

Mom's eyes widened. "A BMW? What in the world is a BMW?"

"Get into the twentieth century, Mom," Mary said. "They're German cars. Tres cool. Not your usual greasy kids' stuff. Rich kids drive 'em. There's a lot of them in Gainesville."

"Really?" Mom said. "Hmmm. Well then if that's what he wants, that's what he'll get. How much do these greasy kids' cars cost?"

"She said rich kids, Mom, not greasy kids," I told her. "About thirty thousand, give or take."

"Oh," Mom said. And then, "What? Did you say thirty thousand? You mean dollars? For a car?"

Mary and I both nodded and Mom turned away from us and looked out the window as though we'd made up the price and if she didn't look at us it might come down.

"You're sure about that?" she asked, slowly turning back to face us.

Again we nodded.

"So be it," she said with just a little puff of a sigh. "Why not? Thirty thousand can't be any harder to materialize than thirty, can it?"

"About twenty-nine thousand, nine hundred and seventy harder, I'd say," Mary said, picking up a magazine and flipping through the pages as though, as far as she was concerned, the conversation was over.

It wasn't over for Mom though and she turned her full attention on me. "It's a deal then, right? One bright red WMB coming up."

"BMW," I corrected.

"Whatever... We'll surprise him with it for graduation! Can you imagine his face when he sees it! How'll we give it to him? I mean, we can't just *give* it to him. We've got to *sock* it to him. Make an event out of it. None of this parking it in the driveway with a bow on top, or putting the keys in a cute little box, kind of nonsense."

"How are you going to come up with thirty thousand?" came Mary's voice, like doom, from the couch.

"Something will come to me, Mary," Mom said, exasperated at the interruption. "I'll get a hunch. An intuition. And I'm not going to get bogged down on the money angle anymore than I did when I got my horse. Or the carpeting. What if..? No. Let's see... What if we park it outside his dorm, with his name on top? So if he looked out the window he'd see it?"

"Wouldn't work," I said. "There's too many Steves in the world and even if it flew right up to the fourth floor and hit him in the face, he wouldn't think it was for him. What if..."

"Knock it off, you two," Mary growled, jumping up from the couch and throwing the magazine aside. "You're being ridiculous, Mom, and you know it. You sound like Scarlet O'Hara with your, 'I'll think of something,' You don't even have thirty dollars never mind thirty thousand, so where do you think you'll find the rest? Not counting tax, of course. And Steve doesn't expect a car. All you're doing is dreaming."

"You don't have to say it as though the zeroes go off into eternity, Mary. After all, what are zeroes anyway but little empty holes? And it's about time we started dreaming. And dreaming big. Why should all the good stuff go to other people? We need to change the way we see ourselves, that's all. At least, I do. We'll start with Steve's car and go on from there. So, let's see. If he graduates next May, that gives us a good eleven months to make it happen. Plenty of time..."

That's what gets me when I'm in the middle of Mom and Mary arguing. They both make sense though I'd never let

Mary know I thought that. The way Mom put it, like it was as easy as going out to buy the week's groceries, I wondered how come we hadn't bought Steve a car a long time ago. And then I turn around and there's Mary looking mad as all, shaking her head and saying thirty thousand like the zeroes went off into forever and I think, Yeah, how could Mom ever get hold of that kind of money? Her head has to be full of rocks.

"So how are we going to get the money?" I asked, hoping Mom could come up with something that would shut Mary up and get her off our backs.

And then it's Mom who's scowling and looking so like Mary I wondered if she hadn't been more like her when she was a kid than she ever lets on. "Is that all you two ever think about? Money? It's ideas we're after."

"I know!" Mary said, turning to me, her eyes widening as though she'd suddenly seen the light. "We'll go get us a How To book and build it ourselves. Out in the garage. After work and on weekends. Right, Mom?"

"No, Mary, we're not going to build one in the garage and don't be sarcastic. It's all so much easier than that. All we have to do is imagine ourselves giving him one. Steve driving it with an ear-splitting grin on his face. The ways and means, the ideas of how to do it, will come by themselves. We're just going to keep our thoughts and attention firmly fixed on that end result."

"Oh, my God! She really is going to pursue this mind stuff," Mary groaned.

"Why wouldn't I? There's no other way. The thought has to come first. When are you going to understand that simple little fact?"

"Never. So give it up. Steve never asked for a car because he knows it's impossible for you to give him one. He's not expecting one."

"All the more reason then, and fun, to give him one. And try to get that word 'impossible' out of your vocabulary, will you? It's really so counter-productive."

"Mo-ther, Mo-ther," Mary sighed. "I hate to see you set yourself up for the biggest disappointment of your life. It's scary. Plus, you're not doing Jeff any favors filling his head up with all this garbage. Leave it alone. Steve'll have his degree soon. He can buy his own car."

"I know he can," Mom said quietly. "But I *want* to give him one. It's a challenge to me. A chance to prove my theory once and for all. It's exciting."

"Why don't you give yourself an easier challenge then? Why don't you just help him with the down payment on a second-hand car? That would be a terrific present. Better than a briefcase or a pen set. He'd be tickled to death."

I thought to myself I'd puke if anyone gave me a briefcase or a pen set, but I didn't say anything.

Mom shook her head. "You still don't understand that this is about more than money, do you? This is about taking a stand, changing ourselves from people who've programmed themselves to think borderline destitution to people who can, and do, live comfortably. It's just too easy to go along as we have in the past, turning away from everything exciting and wonderful, stamping it 'impossible', using our so-called circumstances as an excuse.

"I'm taking a stand now. I'm changing our circumstances because I, for one, am sick to death of living as we do. Of hitting the floor everyday at six a.m. and spending every minute of every day at someone else's beck and call. Of never, ever having enough of anything. I don't choose to live that way anymore and I don't choose to give Steve a second hand car. I want to give him a nice new one. And one he really wants. Why dream little when you can dream big?"

"You just said it, I didn't. And that's all your doing, dreaming. You just don't imagine cars into existence, Mom. If it was that easy how come you're driving a heap? How come everyone in the world isn't driving beautiful cars? How come you didn't dream one up for me? I'd have liked a BMW, too."

"Then why didn't you get yourself one instead of the one you have?"

"I couldn't afford one and you know it," Mary said, looking like she was about to burst into tears. "I didn't know then, of course, that you were in the car-dreaming business or I'd have asked you to get me one."

"You didn't get yourself one, Mary, because you got stuck on 'impossible'. If you'd believed in it, always imagined owning one, seen yourself at the wheel of one, that's what you'd be driving. You settled for less."

"I was being practical," Mary said defensively.

She looked so upset that Mom got up and went and put her arms around her. "I know you were, baby. And you learned that from me. And I'm not saying that being practical is wrong. It's just that maybe we've all been too practical for too long. It's so limiting. And that's what Steve is being up there, too. Practical. And if we leave it to him, when the time comes, he'll buy a practical car and live a practical life and get bogged down. Just like me. He won't dream big. And it's up to us to put a stop to that before it's too late. We're going to start putting a little more faith and trust in ourselves. We'll be a little less practical and a lot more imaginative. I'm going to start right now seeing us as people who naturally drive nice, new cars and go to exciting places and don't fall apart when some jerk steals a stupid bicycle. In fact, I'd like to meet whoever it was that stole that bike. I'd thank him personally for waking me up. About time too. We'll start with Steve's car and go from there. Let's see, if he graduates in May, we've got almost a year to get our act together."

NINE

I don't really know what I expected from Mom after that but I sure expected more than what I saw. I mean, there she'd been, practically promising to pull a really cool car out of thin air and what was she doing? Nothing. Nothing I could see anyway. And I watched her real close for a couple of weeks. All I saw was her going to work same as usual, cooking, doing housework, ironing, sewing, yelling at Mary and me. Everything just like always.

One Saturday when I came in from swim practice she had the sewing machine going full blast and her mouth full of pins like she always does when she sews.

"Thought you weren't making any more of that homemade stuff," I said, remembering how along with everything else, she'd said she was going to see herself elegant in store-bought clothes.

"I'm not," she hissed through her teeth so she wouldn't swallow the pins. "Well, I am, but not for the reason you think."

She gave up trying to talk through the pins and took them out. "The fact is, I'm better at dress-making than I thought. The clothes I make are a lot nicer, and better finished, than the ones I buy. I wasted every lunch hour last week looking for a dress for the Wilson's party tonight and I couldn't find a thing." She grinned. "Do you believe it? Here we are on our way to a whole new lifestyle and I'm still going to have to wear homemade clothes."

Seeing she'd got on the subject herself, I asked as casually as I could, "You figured a way to get Steve a car yet?" In fact, so casual I turned and emptied the contents of the fridge on the counter and started making myself a sandwich so I wouldn't have to look her in the eye. I mean, I guess if there were any doubts going to show up there, I didn't want to see them.

"No. And I don't have to. All I have to do is focus on the end result. It'll come."

"A month has gone by already. You've only got ten left."

"I know. Don't nag. Do you have any idea how much time there is in ten months?"

To tell you the truth, I don't. I've always had a hard time figuring it out. I mean, if I'm looking forward to something like Christmas or my birthday, then ten months seems like forever. But give me two months off school for summer and man, those months are gone like minutes.

"A lot," Mom yelled over the roar of the machine. "Ten months is a lot of time if you use it right."

"So... How're you using it right?"

"Oh..." She ran another seam on the machine pulling the pins out of the material as she went along and sticking them in between her teeth again. "Building it up in my mind. You know, seeing me – us - giving Steve the car he wants, seeing his face... And seeing me freed from earning a living. Maybe getting Mary a car like Steve's if she wants one. You going to college and not having to work like Steve does. Stuff like that."

"Damn!" I said. "I thought we were just going for a car for Steve. You sure are expecting a lot from yourself." And to myself I was thinking how glad I was Mary wasn't there to blow holes in all of it. But thinking, too, how I could really go for that kind of life.

"I'm going over to Rick's," I told Mom when I'd cleaned up the mess from my lunch. "He's going to let me make a CD on his computer."

She nodded, not looking up from her sewing. "Don't be late for dinner. I'm going out tonight."

I was halfway out the door when I heard her call my name.

"I'm going to need your help," she said, when I was back in front of her.

"What for?" I groaned, wishing I'd gotten out of there sooner.

"Nothing hard," she said. "Fun stuff. Why don't we go take a look at this car Steve wants one Saturday?"

"At a dealers, you mean?"

"Yes."

"Heck, yes. We could go now if you want."

She laughed. "No. I've got to finish this dress and you've got to make a tape. But soon, OK?"

"You've got it. But what do you need me for?"

"I'd like to have you with me, that's all. It'll be fun. And I've never bought a car. I won't know what to ask about. They might not take me seriously. It's still a man's world, you know. If I go alone they'll think, Here comes another dumb broad. But if you come with me, I'll look like a mother. You know... Serious."

We went the following Saturday right after breakfast. It was too early for Mary, still in a robe, to come awake enough to give us a lecture. But she didn't need to. Her early morning face was saying, "Give it up," for her.

We parked our heap on a side street by the dealers so, like Mom said, "They won't look down their noses at the poor old thing," and made our way across the lot passing rows of second hand cars, their prices daubed in big white letters on their windshields. Some of them looked pretty cool to me and I would have liked to stop and look them over. "Hey, look at those wheels," I said to Mom, pointing out a dark green Lexus. "Bet Steve would love that. And look, it's only six thousand bucks."

She didn't even look in the direction I pointed. "You want to dream little, Jeff, or big?" was all she tossed over her shoulder as she pushed open the big glass doors of the showroom where the BMWs and other, incredible, imported cars shimmered on a high-gloss floor.

Coming from the heat and busyness of the lot outside, it was as quiet and cool and dim in there as an empty church and the sound of Mom's high heels clacking across those slick floors seemed almost sinful. I wanted to tell her to tiptoe or take her shoes off only I thought my voice might sound as bad as her heels in all that silence.

At first it didn't look like there was anyone in there but us but then I heard a scraping sound and made out a couple of guys sitting at desks behind a glass wall and then one of them was hurrying our way pumping what must have been some kind of breath deodorizer into his mouth as he walked. His pants were high-waters and flapped around his skinny ankles and his blow-dried hair made his head look like a globe a couple sizes too big for the rest of him.

"Oh, dear," Mom murmured, and then the guy was beside us.

"And what can we sell you today, little lady?" he asked, extending his hand to shake Mom's while a crumb from what must've been a donut went up and down on his bottom lip with every word he said.

I could've told him right then that he'd just lost all hope of ever selling Mom anything. Mom is tall and doesn't take kindly to being called little.

"BMW," I whispered, afraid she'd come out with it ass-backwards again.

"A BMW," she said, ignoring the guy's hand and drawing herself up so that she looked across the top of his puffy hair. "In red," she added, like she was buying shoes.

"Sure, sure," the guy said, spreading his arms wide to take in every car on the floor. "That's what we sell, BMWs.

'Fraid we don't have a red one on the lot right now but I can get one for you right quick. What kind of car you driving now?"

"I'm not going to tell you," Mom said, all uppity, as though she had a Rolls parked out there on the side street.

She walked slowly towards the nearest car, frowning. "They're awfully small for such expensive cars, aren't they?"

I felt myself turning red and wishing I'd stayed home as she pulled up in front of a Mercedes and stooped to peer inside.

The sales guy put his hand up to his mouth to hide his smile. He felt the crumb and it was his turn to feel like a jerk.

I touched Mom's arm. "That's not a BMW," I hissed, and pointed to the nearest car that was. "That is."

Mom straightened and sauntered towards it. "They're so small," she said again, sounding whiney, while looking at a seven series.

The sales guy caught up with us. "The trend these days, little lady, is towards smaller cars," he said, opening the car door and motioning Mom to get in. "And I guarantee if you sit in it you'll find it very roomy inside."

Mom installed herself behind the wheel and, not knowing what else to do, turned the steering wheel a little each way and studied all the knobs and buttons and opened and closed the ash tray. "It smells very nice in here," she said brightly, beaming us a big smile.

"Nothing like the smell of a new car," the guy agreed.

"This isn't the model Steve wants," I said loudly before Mom could make any more dumb remarks. "He wants a 325i, like that white one over there by the window."

"So he does," Mom beamed, glad of an excuse to get out of the car she was in.

"The little lady did say a big car," the guy reproved, helping her disentangle herself from the deep cushions of the seven series and steering her towards the other car.

"So this is what Steve wants," Mom said, stalking the white 325i from every angle. "I wonder why?"

Both the sales guy and I started talking at once, me all exasperated, him all superior.

"It's a cool car, Mom. Come on! Anybody can see that."

"The BMW is the finest example of automotive engineering ever to come out of Germany."

"Well, maybe if I test drove it, I'd understand." Mom shrugged.

"Mom, you don't need to drive it," I said, forgetting we didn't have a dime. "Just buy it!"

Mom looked really shocked. "I wouldn't dream of buying a car without driving it first, Jeff. Good heavens, what kind of a fool do you take me for? Steve would never forgive me if we showed up with a car that might... Well... perform poorly in some way."

"Steve?" the Salesman pounced. "Who's Steve? I mean, it always helps to know who the owner's gonna be. Matching types, you know."

"Steve?" Mom said absently-mindedly. "Why, Steve is..." she paused and I saw a little smile come and go across her face, "...my boy friend," she finished looking straight at me, daring me to laugh. I didn't. I was too busy thinking how I'd like to strangle her and wishing, for once in my life, Mary was there to shut her up before she really got going. They would have heard her, "Oh, my God!" clear across town.

"... and he'll be twenty-two next birthday and I want to give him the car of his dreams." Mom finished.

"Then, little lady, you oughta give him the biggest car we got, being it's such a special present for such a... uh... special kind of guy," the salesman said and I gave him one for not missing a beat.

"Steve definitely told me he wanted a 325i," I said, before Mom could embarrass me again.

"Yes, he did," Mom agreed. "I heard him," and a really big grin settled on her face. "You know kids! They're all crazy about these funny little cars. They tell me Gainesville's just full of them."

"Yeah? Could be. Don't get up Gainesville way much myself. And this, uh... Steve. He wants a red one, huh?"

"Yes. Bright red."

"Well, like I said, we don't got none on hand right now. Could have one here inside a week though."

"No need," Mom said airily. "We've got eight months before the big day. Plenty of time."

"Eight months!" the guy spluttered.

"Yes. No hurry. We'll just take a little test drive in one that's handy and then we won't take up any more of your time."

"But, lady! You're talking close on a year! No sense driving one now if you're not taking delivery for a year. And... fact is, I'm kind've busy right now."

"I'm busy all the time." Mom said firmly. "I might not be able to get away in eight months. We'll do it now."

The salesman sighed and went squishing off across the floor in his rubber soled shoes with a glance at the guys behind the glass wall that seemed to beg for understanding. Mom clattered along behind him and I brought up the rear trying to decide whether or not to go along on the test drive. I decided, what the heck, it'd be fun to tell Steve I'd been in one and then I remembered I couldn't tell Steve anything at all about this car stuff. Not if we were going to surprise him. Not that I was sure Mom would ever get him one and, man, I got myself so confused I hardly heard any of the stuff the guy was saying about the car while Mom drove it. I know she made me sit up front with her and kept squeezing my knee, knowing, I guess, that I wasn't feeling any too happy about the way things had gone all morning.

"Why'd you do that?" I asked her when we were back in our own car. "Tell the guy Steve was your boy friend?"

"I'm not really sure," she sighed. "And I'm sorry I embarrassed you. I think I must have wanted to throw him off before he started asking questions about down payments and monthly payments and dreary things like that. I wanted him to think I was an airhead who couldn't talk sense if I tried."

"He did."

"I know. Doesn't matter though. When we really go out to buy one we'll go someplace else. Not back there. I even embarrassed myself. And if you don't want to come next time you don't have to. Anyway, next time I'll know more about those funny looking cars than all those salesmen put together."

I wasn't about to take bets on that so I said, "They are cool cars."

"Yes, they are. And fun to drive, too. Especially after this poor old baby. Don't you think I drove it quite nicely?"

"That poor guy in the back seat didn't seem too impressed."

"How was I supposed to know they put reverse in a different place?"

"He told you."

"He did? I didn't hear him. Anyway, I only bumped that trash can. I didn't knock it over."

"It could have been a person."

"Stop it, Jeff! Why make me nervous about something that's over and done with. Anyway, I won't be driving it. Steve will."

"Now we've done it, I'm trying to remember why we went there today when we're not ready to buy. Why didn't you wait until we were? That was a nightmare back there."

"I know. I was going to wait only I was having a hard time imagining Steve driving it and being happy with it when I didn't even know what they looked like. I needed to see one up close and touch it and sit in it. Now it'll be a lot easier. It'll help if you imagine it all too."

"Imagine what, exactly?"

"Us doing what we did this morning. Only see us driving away in it. A red one, of course. And then imagine us giving it to Steve. See the expression on his face. The whole thing."

"I don't know..." I began.

"What is there to know?"

"I don't know if I believe in all this stuff." I said. "You just make it all sound too easy."

"It is easy. Stop trying to make it hard. I'll prove it to you. The lesson is that you get what you think about, right? OK, then, right now we've got to stop at the supermarket. You know what their parking lot is like on a Saturday morning. I'm going to park right up by the front door."

"This I gotta see," I said, and meant it. In our town nobody in their right mind shops on Saturday mornings and I couldn't hardly believe Mom was going to try. The parking lot is always jammed with frustrated shoppers inching along in their cars, bumper to bumper, waiting and watching for someone to leave. Only nobody ever does. I've seen more accidents in that parking lot than out on the Interstate.

"In my mind," Mom said dramatically, "I see an empty parking space right up by the front door. Not another cruiser in sight. It's ours."

"Show me, Little Lady," I said as we pulled into the lot and maneuvered into line behind all the other cars weaving in and out of the lanes between the parking slots.

"I imagine it in the very center section," Mom said, passing up several outer lanes that could have had a parking space in them.

"You better get in line then," I said. "There's about ten cars up ahead of you. All with the same idea."

"Yes, but the difference between them and me is that I *know* I will park there, I insist upon it, and they don't think they have a prayer," Mom said, turning into the center lane. She no sooner said that than the brake lights on a parked car lit up and it started backing out, an inch at a time. "Back up quick," I said, hardly believing our luck. "Let him out. You've got it."

Mom shook her head. "I said right up by the front door and that's what I meant."

"Be for real, Mom. Park. I believe you, OK? We'll be here all day if you don't."

I might as well have been talking to the windshield. She just kept on going and damn me if right before we got to the very end car, the one right next to the handicapped space in front of the door, than two kids come flying towards it, jump in and take off like they'd been caught shop lifting. Mom pulled into the space.

"Do I make my point?" she said, looking at me sideways and trying not to gloat.

"Lucky," I said. "You got lucky, is all."

"Not lucky at all. Just believing the impossible is possible, is all."

"Mom, finding parking spaces for cars is cool but it doesn't impress me that much," I told her. "But the day you walk into a BMW showroom and drive out at the wheel of a 325i, that's the day I'll really believe you. I mean, *really* believe you."

Mom stuck out her hand for me to shake. "Deal?"

"Deal," I said, and I took her hand and shook it thinking, Man, if she ever pulls that one off, I'll believe everything she ever tells me for the rest of my life.

Ten

When you live in Florida and the sun shines every day, it's pretty hard to keep track of holidays. I mean, when you have the same kind of weather at Easter as you do at Thanksgiving, they kind of sneak up on you. At least now I'm getting older they do. When I was a little kid, I'd start getting excited about Christmas as soon as we went back to school in September and it didn't matter to me what the weather was like. I guess part of it, too, is that when you get older, you get busier and you don't have so much time to sit around and daydream. At least I know I don't and I miss it.

That's how it was the year I'm talking about. I was nearly through with high school by then, busy with track and swim team and trying to beat Steve's high-school record of Honor Roll every semester by making the Dean's List every one. I didn't have much choice. Every time he wrote he said he'd beat my scumbag butt if I didn't do better than him.

Like I really needed him telling me that! I'd planned on beating him way back when I was in first grade.

Anyway, along with my school stuff and getting at least one detention a week for talking in class, and helping around the house and earning what money I could and hanging out with my friends – "the animals" - Mary called them, it was suddenly Thanksgiving and Steve was home.

Always when he walks through the door, his head nearly hitting the frame he's so tall, it's like he's just been down the block and not away for months. Mom notices it too. "If Steve went away for twenty years," she says, "and then came walking through the door, we'd just pick up right where we left off. As though we'd had breakfast together and now it's lunch time. Time doesn't come into it."

"Hey," I said, helping him carry his gear to his room. "Guess what Mom and I did the other day? We test..."

"You test what...?"

"Uh... nothing." I fumbled. "That is, I gave her a test. We were over at the shopping center and you know how she's always saying you get what you think about? Well, I told her to think about parking right up by the front door. The place was packed. It was a Saturday..."

"Quit stalling. What happened?"

"She did it. I couldn't believe it. 'Course," I hurried on in case he thought I was losing it, "she just got lucky. That's what I told her."

"I wouldn't be so sure," he said, throwing himself on to his bed with a big, satisfied sigh. "I think she's on to something."

"You do?"

"Yep. I've been trying it myself and it works."

"Like what?" was all I could think to say. I mean, he didn't have a car did he?

"School stuff mostly. Like this semester I had some really tough courses, plus they gave me more hours on the job than I thought I could handle. Man, I was frantic. I was about to drop a class when I thought about Mom's ideas and I figured I'd try them for a couple of weeks. I stopped seeing myself so darn overwhelmed. So rushed. Stopped seeing the courses so tough. Saw myself with a couple A's. A lot of free time."

"And...?"

"It worked. I got exactly what I thought about. My classes are easy. The A's are rolling in. And I have a ton of time both for study and the job. Plus I've been to more parties this semester than in all my other years combined. It's unreal! I got to thinking then about other years when I'd made it work the other way. Worrying about hours, about not getting from one class to another on time, not having time to study, about being late for work and getting fired and never getting enough sleep and never seeing my friends or going to parties. God! All I ever did was worry. And I got exactly what I thought about. My whole life was a nightmare."

Hearing it from Steve was a whole other thing than hearing it from Mom. Man, he had me so excited I shivered.

"I'm gonna try it," I said. "But... I still don't see how it works. I mean, it makes me feel like a dorky little kid believing in magic."

"Nothing magic about it. Thought creates everything, both the world as we know it and the way we see ourselves. Just look around you. You'll soon see everybody on the planet lives it. You'll see the worriers, like I was, afraid to let up on themselves because if they do they might not make a passing grade. And that's all they ever get, a passing grade. Then there's the opposite, guys that show up late for class, if they show at all, then sleep through it when they do. 'No sweat, man,' they say when you remind them exams are tomorrow. 'I'll scrape by. I always do.' And they do! And you should watch the athletes! The champions. Those guys are so fired up they couldn't think about anything but excelling in their sport if they tried. If you could open up their heads you'd see movies going on in there. Movies of themselves playing the star, the hero. The winner!

"Same thing with the real brains. The triple A students. Those guys just burn to 'know'. They see themselves knowing, having all the answers. And they do, because it's all they think about. Mom's right. You do get what you think about. You can't escape it even if you wanted to. Believe it. You're doing it anyhow."

"I will," I said, "I will!" And in my head I saw my report card, a blur of beautiful A's and Mom laughing and patting me on the back. And I saw my swim coach running towards me waving his stop watch, yelling, "You did it! You broke the school record!" and Mom and Mary screeching like cats in the bleachers.

Sheelagh Mawe

"Heck," I said, "All this stuff is, is worrying in reverse. Instead of filling my head up with what if I don't get an A? Or, what if I don't even qualify for the next meet, I'll just reverse it and think about how I'll feel when I've done it."

"Go for it," he said, giving me a high five. "Amaze me."

"I'm gonna. But... I've been remembering that old movie we saw one time on TV," I said, "You know, that real funny one, *The Secret Life of Walter Mitty*."

He nodded.

"Well, that guy was always imagining himself doing really neat stuff, but in the end he was always just dumb old Walter. It didn't work for him."

Steve thought about that a minute, then said, "That's because one minute he was imagining he was a riverboat gambler or a fighter pilot, the next he was back in his real life office. He wasn't using his imagination for day-to-day living. He was using it to escape day-to-day living."

"Yeah, I see what you mean. OK. I'm going to give it a whirl," I started to laugh. "You might be sorry though," I said, remembering how I'd already decided to do everything better than him.

"How come?"

"I might be... Well, maybe I'll get better at some stuff than you."

"If you do it right, you will." he said, grinning. "It'll all come down to who's got the best grip on his own imagination."

"Watch me," I said. "Just watch me."

You want to know something? It works! Does for me anyway. First thing I tried it on was algebra. Algebra had always been a tough one for me. The hardest thing I'd come across since I was four years old and trying to fly like Superman. But after Thanksgiving and my talk with Steve, I started seeing myself sitting in class, my mind right there and not wandering off someplace it didn't belong, understanding every word the teacher said and knowing the answers before he even got to them. And then I saw myself streaming through my homework, doing it all in minutes instead of the hours it usually took.

It wasn't long before everything started coming so easy I had to remind myself that I really was in school, my hand up, knowing the answers and not in the middle of a daydream. It nearly blew my mind. I mean, damn, it was all so simple. Simple and sort of clean and neat.

"Inevitable" is what Mom called it when I told her about it. "As in, the way of the universe," she clarified.

"You mean the math or the imagining?"

"Both," she said. "Both. Keep it up and you'll have the world by the tail."

"It's got nothing to do with imagining," Mary said. "The kid got As because he started paying attention and kept his stupid mouth shut for once in his life."

"Why don't you try keeping your mouth shut for the rest of your life?" I asked her.

"It would please me very much if you'd both keep your mouths shut, at least until we've finished dinner," Mom said, interrupting our glares.

"I'm trying it on swim team next," I said.

"You should," Mary said sweetly, "If you keep your mouth shut under water long enough, maybe we'll get lucky and you'll blow up."

"I keep imagining that someday you two will learn to get along," Mom sighed, standing up to clear the table, "but some things stagger the most vivid imagination."

By Christmas, when Steve was home again - and remember I'd only had about three weeks to work in - I had a whole mess of things I'd improved on to tell him about. "Algebra's a breeze," I told him. "So are the rest of my classes. I've knocked a whole 5 seconds off the 500 meters and Coach says if I keep it up I'll break the school record come spring. I've bought the whole family really cool Christmas presents and don't even ask where the money came from. I just saw myself having it when I needed it and there's a ton more coming from putting up people's outdoor Christmas lights. And I've got time to daydream again. That's the best part, the day-dreaming. Man, it's like I sit down and close my eyes and picture myself with whatever I want and next thing I know I'm out there and it's all happening."

"What'd I tell you?"

"I know. You told me. But... how come everyone doesn't do it?"

"They do! I told you that too, remember? Trouble is, most of them spend their whole lives imagining all the bad stuff that could happen to them. So that's what they get. They'll tell you so themselves. 'I had a feeling when I got up this morning,' they say, 'that everything was going to go wrong.' So it does. Or they'll say something like, 'My Dad's been talking all along about how he might lose his job and I'd have to drop out of school. Well, he lost it, so I guess I won't be seeing you for a semester or two. If ever...'"

"Why don't you tell them to stop talking and thinking like that?"

He snorted. "I've tried. They look at me like I'm crazy. Get mad, even. Like we did when Mom first started telling us about it. Like Mary still does. They don't want to believe they're the ones making it happen. It's too much responsibility for them. It's a lot easier to blame their troubles on fate or the roll of the dice or some such. You tried telling anyone about it?"

"Heck, no," I said. "You think I'm stupid or something? Then everyone would be beating me at everything I'm trying to do myself. I'd never break the school record in the five hundred."

"Dummy. It doesn't work like that at all. Not everyone in the world wants to break the five hundred meters or be good in algebra. Everybody has their own goals."

"Yeah? Well how about the other guys on the swim team? The ones that do swim the five hundred and want to break records as bad as me?"

"That's easy enough for you to have figured out for yourself," he said. "Obviously if you've got two guys going for the same thing, then the one who holds onto the end result and refuses to think fear thoughts, like, 'I hope I get off to a good start,' or, 'I hope I don't lose ground on my turns today,' or, 'I hope the other kids screw up,' is the guy that wins. Your winner doesn't "hope" anything. He *knows* it's him making it happen. He knows he's not at the mercy of anything but what he lets in his own head."

"Damn," I said, and I remember feeling excited and happy about what I could go for in my life. "Do you suppose there's people around who know about this and use it all the time?"

"You better believe it. Anybody who's achieved anything in life uses it, though some of them might not know it consciously. But they're all people who had a dream, who saw themselves succeeding regardless of the obstacles or the opinions of others who laughed and jeered at them. Otherwise, they wouldn't be where they are. As for people doing it on purpose? You bet there are. Heck, if Mom found it in a book, other people have, too. Hundreds and thousands of them, maybe. But how're you ever gonna know? You try to explain it to someone who seems to be having a hard time, tell them that their own thinking is causing all their problems, and they look at you like you're out to lunch. They firmly believe that everything that happens to them is out of their control. So guess what?"

"Their lives are out of control," I said.

"You're catching on," he said. "And that's why you can't get through to them. They *think* we're nuts. I know. I've tried."

We had the best Christmas that year of any I can remember. Everything we'd asked Mom for and she'd said a flat NO to, was there under the tree Christmas morning.

"How'd you do it?" we gasped as one wonder after another came out of the mess of boxes and tissue.

"I'll give you three guesses," she said sleepily, staring around at our grinning faces and the piles of presents. "This year I just thought 'Yes' instead of 'No' and here it all is. I don't owe a penny on any of it either. It's all paid for."

"You're the greatest, Mom," Mary said, stomping around in the boots she'd been eating her heart out for ever since I can remember. "Even if you do think weird."

"Don't knock it till you've tried it," Steve warned.

"Too bad you don't try thinking yourself once in a while," I told her. "Regular or weird."

"Shut up," Mary said.

"If you're going to get into it this morning, I'm walking out," Mom warned. "In a couple of hours this house is going to be full of people. Your friends as well as mine, so let's move it. And you two will please not speak to each other for the rest of the day."

The whole Christmas holiday was like that. People coming to our house, us going to theirs and Mom, when she wasn't at work, not letting Mary and me talk to each other. It worked out great.

We took the tree down during commercials New Year's Day and then Steve left and I went back to school and got busy imagining myself up at the top of all my classes and it was the end of February before I even thought about Steve's car and this being his next to last semester. I guess I freaked.

"Steve's graduating in three months," I babbled into the phone as soon as Mom picked up at her end.

"That's right," her voice came sing-songing back along the wires.

"What about the money? For the car?" I asked urgently.

"What money?"

"What are you doing about it, is what about it. Have you got any money?"

"I seem to remember saying we wouldn't get bogged down on the money side of it," she said. "But actually, yes, I do."

Good old Mom, I thought, feeling myself relax all over. She's coming through just like she said she would.

"That's cool," I sighed, grinning like she was there in front of me.

"Two hundred dollars," her voice trilled.

I closed my eyes to stop myself falling off the kitchen counter where I like to balance whenever I use the phone. She is crazy, I thought. Mary's been right all along. Out loud I said, "Two hundred bucks?" and my voice was shaking I was so mad. "That's all? Jeez, that won't even buy a door handle. You're crazy, Mom. All this time and all you've got is two hundred crummy dollars? Steve graduates in May, you know."

"I'm aware of that fact, Jeff," Mom's voice came back, all the trills gone and ice in its place.

"But Mom... You said... We made a deal, remember? We shook on it."

Mom's voice thawed and she said, "I know we did, honey, and I'm working on it. I'll have another couple of hundred in no time at all and we'll just keep on going from there."

That time I took the phone away from my ear and shook it, wondering if maybe there wasn't something wrong with it. Something that was keeping me from hearing right. And then I sat staring at it, thinking maybe she just plain doesn't know, doesn't understand, the difference between two hundred or two thousand or twenty thousand. The way girls at school squeal and carry on when it comes time for math and say they can't do it and don't understand it, and what do they need to know math for anyway? Maybe, I thought, maybe there's something in females' heads that honest-to-God can't put two and two together and maybe my Mom has a real bad case of it.

"Jeff?" Mom's voice crackled in the receiver in my hand and I quick put it up to my ear.

"I'm here, Mom."

"Stop worrying. Everything's going to be fine."

"Oh, I'm not worrying." I said, thinking, Just sick is all.

"Good. I'll explain everything when I get home, OK?"

"OK."

I hung up the phone thinking that's going to be some explanation: two hundred bucks for a thirty thousand dollar car. And how this was another one of those times when she definitely made me feel like I was the grown up and she was the kid and what in the world was I supposed to do with her?

ELEVEN

I didn't leave my room and my homework when I heard Mom come in from work that day but waited, listening for the sounds of her going to her room where I knew she would change, then for the rattle of pots and pans and running water in the kitchen so I would know she was starting dinner. I waited a bit longer till I knew she had everything going and was probably going through the mail before I went out and said, "Hi". I had a pencil and a notebook with me so I could show her, very clearly, that you cannot buy a BMW with a couple hundred dollars. I even stuck my calculator in my back pocket in case she didn't understand what I wrote.

"About Steve's car..." I began, crossing the room and settling myself on a bar stool across the counter from her.

"What about it?" she said, not looking up from the mail she was going through. Then she remembered. "That's right," she said. "We said we'd talk about it tonight. Well," she set the mail aside and smiled, "Guess what? After we talked this afternoon, I checked out our finances and juggled a few things around and I'm going to be able to put another seventy-five dollars aside this month. Isn't that great?"

This isn't going to be easy, I thought, looking at her face, all eager, waiting for me to agree with her.

"Yeah, sure," I said. "That's great. Seventy-five dollars is a lot of money," and carefully, in big letters, I wrote a dollar sign on my paper and followed it with the numbers seven and five, a decimal point and two zeros. "And you already had two hundred dollars, right?" I looked up at her and she nodded, her eyes following my hand, watching me write two hundred and another decimal point and two more zeros under the seventy-five. Carefully, I drew a line under the two sets of figures and wrote the total under them, underlining it with a double line. "So now you've got two hundred seventy-five, right?" I looked up at her again and she was nodding, but looking kind of impatient too.

"OK," I went on, "and a Beemer costs thirty thousand dollars, give or take a few bucks, right?" And I wrote that in large letters above the two seventy-five, making sure I got in all the zeros and that she saw every one of them. "Now if we subtract what you've got from what you need, you'll see you are short..." I did the subtraction for her and said, "Twenty-nine thousand, seven hundred and twenty-five dollars to be exact." Softly I repeated the numbers and added, "In three months, Mom. Three months."

I was afraid to look at her then. I mean, there it was, in black and white. She had to understand. I waited for her to say something but she didn't so I made myself look up and she was frowning, her eyes going back and forth from the numbers to me.

Finally, in a voice that was trying hard to be patient, she said, "Jeff, what exactly are you getting at?"

"What I'm getting at," I said, also trying hard to be patient, "is that you've got less than three months to come up with this amount," I drew a circle around the $29,725. "and it's taken you since last October to get this two hundred seventy-five dollars." I stopped then because she made a funny noise like a hiccup and covered her face with her hands.

Damn, I thought, watching her shoulders shake, now I've done it. Out loud I said, "It's nothing to cry over, Mom. Lots of people can't add or subtract." I reached out and patted her shoulder. "And it's not like Steve knows about the car or anything. Heck, nobody knows but us. So big deal. You tried."

She took her hands away from her face then and I saw she wasn't crying at all. She was laughing. Laughing so hard the tears were running down her face. It took her a while to stop and I had to go get some Kleenex so she could mop herself up and all the while I was wondering what was going on in her head that was so damn funny and whether it was just her or whether all women's heads worked the same way and I tell you it was like one of us lived on earth and the other on some far distant planet and what I couldn't figure was, was it her or me that lived on the planet?

"I'm sorry, honey," she gasped when at last she had breath to speak. "I do worry you, don't I? I'm so sorry. This is supposed to be a wonderful surprise we're planning and instead of making it fun for you I've worried you half sick. I really am sorry." And it was her turn to reach over the counter and pat my shoulder.

"As for this," she pointed to the $29,725 circled on my paper, "I should have explained sooner. But...it just seemed so obvious, after all we've been through over the years and what we've said, that you'd have realized there's no way I'm going to try and save up all that money. Good Lord, Jeff, no wonder you're looking at me as though I've lost my mind. We'd never get the car if I tried to do that. No. All I'm going for is a few hundred dollars, maybe a thousand, between now and April."

"But, Mom..." I began, but her hand came up and covered my mouth lightly so I couldn't finish.

"No. Be quiet. Just for a minute. Let me explain. I know that would only buy a head light. Well, let's be generous, maybe two. But that's not what we're going to do."

"No? Well, what exactly is it *you* are going to do?"

"I thought I'd told you. In fact, I know I did. I said it was about changing the way we see ourselves. That old self-image thing we talked about way back when Mary changed the way I look."

"You're rambling, Mom!"

"Am I? Sorry. What I'm trying to say is that one of the biggest hurdles most people face when they're making a big change, going from here to there, so to speak, is in overcoming the gap between where they are and where they want to be. It takes a big leap of faith for someone say, weighing in at three hundred pounds, to see themselves at a hundred and thirty. I mean, the physical evidence gets in their way."

"Sorry, I don't get the connection. What's that got to do with us?"

"Well, our physical evidence is – was – that my checking account was permanently stalled on zero."

"So?"

"So that was making it hard for me to see myself as the kind of person who could ever buy - never mind give away - a BMW."

"That's what Mary and I have been trying to tell you all along," I said, feeling both relieved and disappointed she'd been able to figure out that much. I mean if she was going to get practical again – and that's what she was sounding like to me - then where was the car coming from?

"What you have to do," she went on before I could ask, "to get from here to there, is make an act of faith."

"You do? Like what?"

"For me, along with visualizing the end result, of course - us giving Steve the car - is to get myself a few hundred dollars in the bank. That way I instantly go from seeing myself as a poor hand-to-mouth, pitiful kind of drone to," she straightened, gave her head a little toss, "a woman of means. A woman with money in the bank."

I sat there staring at her face for a long time while a million questions zapped through my head like flash bulbs and I couldn't bring myself to ask a single one. I guess I didn't want to hear the answers. I mean, who would? In the end, though, I had to ask a few and I began, "Like... Are you crazy? What...? How can you believe that by putting a few measly bucks in the bank you're going to get Steve a car?"

And all the while my questions were tumbling out, I could hear my voice going up higher and higher and it bugged the hell out of me. I grabbed up my paper with the neat little numbers on it and ripped it in half. "I thought you couldn't add or subtract, Mom," I said, purposely pitching my voice low, "but now I don't think there's a brain in there at all."

She didn't answer me for a while, just sat staring out the window and when she finally did speak, her voice was so low I could hardly hear her. "Thoughts attract, Jeff, like magnets. I've already told you that. Like attracts like. We're living proof. All I've ever thought, the only way I ever saw us, was as this struggling little family trying to make the best of an unfortunate situation. I saw us as victims. But I'm changing all that. It was just an opinion, after all. An attitude. We're not victims. We can do and be anything we want to do or be. And I'm proving it. I'm not broke. I've got money in the bank." She squeezed my hand. "Coming up with five hundred... a thousand... dollars of my own, money I can spend any way I want, throw away if I feel like it, is an act of faith. It's my way of showing myself, proving to myself, that I'm already the kind of woman I want to be."

"We're going to give Steve that car, Jeff," she went on so softly my scalp prickled and the angry words in my head faded away. "I've imagined us giving it to him so many times it's as though the stage has been set and we're the actors. All we have to do is show up and play our roles. It's going to happen. I'm committed. I won't take no for an answer."

"But... It doesn't make sense. Like, where are you going to show up, huh? Where's this stage you're talking about? How'd you ever dream all this up?"

Again she shrugged. "That's what dreaming's all about, Jeff. It's about creating. Setting goals. Believing anything's possible. And I've already told you, we're *not* going to get hung up on the money. If we think everything hinges on money, we're limiting ourselves. The car can come in a million different ways. Like the way we got the carpeting. Like I got my horse. That book. I mean, we just have to know what it is we want and then expect it."

"Expect what?" Mary said, coming in through the inside garage door.

I couldn't believe we hadn't heard her car coming in. From the look on her face, Mom couldn't either.

"So? What are you expecting?" Mary persisted when neither of us answered.

"We were just talking about Steve's car," Mom said with a look at me that said, might as well get it over with.

"Oh, brother," Mary groaned. "You mean, you're into thinking those wacky thoughts again. I thought you'd have gotten over that by now. Do you suppose if I went out and came back in again, we could change the subject?" She got herself a diet Coke from the fridge. "No? Oh, well. So how much have you imagined so far? Five bucks?"

"It's not necessarily about money," I said defensively, feeling, like I always did, that I had to stick up for Mom when Mary's around. "Anyway, she's got two hundred, seventy-five dollars."

"Two hundred seventy-five dollars," Mary marveled. "My, my! About the price of an ash tray in a BMW wouldn't you say?"

She pulled up a stool beside me at the counter so I got up and went around and sat on Mom's side.

Mary put her hands up to her hair so Mom would think she was fixing it and shot me a double bird before turning her attention back to Mom.

"I saw that, Mary," Mom said. "Very juvenile."

"Sounds to me like you're coming up short on two fronts," Mary said. "Imagination and dollars."

"Actually, I'm not," Mom said airily. "I'm doing very well on both counts, thank you. I've imagined every detail of us giving Steve the car of his dreams to the point it's a given. And secondly, I've changed the way I see myself and for the first time since the divorce I'm well on my way to having a thousand in the bank. It's a nice feeling."

"Yeah," I said, jumping in quick before Mary could pull herself together and start screaming at us. "See. It's a done deal. We're going to attract it to us. Like we're some kind of magnets!"

"Magnets," Mary moaned, clapping both hands to her face and looking up at the ceiling. "Did you hear them, Lord? They think they're going to attract a thirty-thousand dollar car." Slowly she withdrew her hands and stared at us, her head swinging from side to side like it had a metronome in it. "That is the dumbest, the absolute dumbest, thing I've ever heard. Steve would go nuts if he knew you were filling Jeff's head up with this kind of crap, Mom. He'd be coming off the walls. It's like you're trying to teach him to believe in Santa Claus and the tooth fairy all over again." Her eyes went upwards again as though she had a friend up there in the ceiling who agreed with everything she said.

Mom shook her head. "Not at all. It's simply that as you have told me so many, many times, I know I have to change myself inwardly if I want things around me to change outwardly and I've done it."

But Mary was not about to let Mom get launched on her theory when she had a theory of her own to scream about.

"Forget it, Momma. You can believe and imagine all you want, but to try and use all that crap and tell Jeff you're going to magnetize an expensive car is pure b.s. and if you weren't so far out in space, you'd know it. Why don't you just give Steve a couple hundred dollars? He'd think he died and went to heaven. He's never seen that kind of money and," she stabbed a fake finger nail at Mom, "neither have you. Why don't you spend it on yourself, for heaven's sake. Or around here? Besides," she paused, her eyes narrowing, "you don't even have five hundred."

"No, but I will," Mom said in that quiet, certain way and I thought to myself, Yeah, darn right! So how come, if I know she can get together five hundred, is it so hard for me to believe the rest? It could happen. I started feeling better.

"So..." Mary began again on a big intake of breath, but Mom held up her hands, shook her head, her eyes saying that's enough, and then yelped and dived for one of the pots on the stove that was belching black smoke.

It took a while to clean up the mess, everyone saying it was everyone else's fault, and we finished up having scrambled eggs for dinner because all the stuff in the other pots was past the eating stage, and we didn't get back on the subject of Steve's car that night.

In fact, a few days went by, the way days do, with all of us crashing off to school and work and only seeing each other at dinner, before the subject came up again. Mary brought it up asking a question that I thought made a lot of sense, especially when you considered the source. The question was: "Why, if you believe you can magnetize a car, can't you magnetize a thousand dollars as well?"

"Because I was looking for an act of faith and a thousand dollars in my bank account, put there by my own determination, was what came to mind when I first started thinking about it," Mom said.

"Oh, my God," Mary groaned. "And I suppose this all came in a vision? There was a blinding light and celestial music and the voice of God saying, 'Susan Martin, get thee one thousand big ones and thou shalt be provided for.'"

"Actually, no," Mom said, dead serious. "It was more like some little people about this big," she held up her hand with the thumb and forefinger about three inches apart. "They were sitting on the front porch one morning when I ran out to pick up the paper."

"Be serious, Mom," I said, hoping to God she wasn't.

"I am, I am. They were the nicest little people you'd ever want to meet and very well dressed. The men all in cutaway suits and top hats, the ladies in beautiful crinoline gowns. Old fashioned, but elegant. Said they'd come to tell me to get one thousand dollars together and they'd take it from there."

"Mo-ther," Mary gasped, her voice squeaking up on the second syllable as though it was breaking like mine and looking so worried I swear she turned pale, "Stop it."

"OK," Mom laughed. "But you started it with your voice of God nonsense. All I'm telling you is I had an idea, just like any perfectly normal person who faces a challenge and looks for ways to overcome it. It's all perfectly clear to me and I'm going to follow it through."

"It's about as clear to me as a pile of mud," Mary spat.

"It doesn't have to be clear to you," Mom told her with a lot of finality. "It's my idea and my thousand dollars and I'm going to give Steve a car."

T WELVE

Looking back now at how hard it was for Mom to get the rest of her thousand bucks together, I'm surprised she ever stuck it out. And the way she went about it really had me scratching my head. I mean, none of it fit in with all her talk about getting what you think about or changing how she saw herself. Coming up with that money was one of the hardest things I ever saw her do. It was nickels and dimes all the way.

We wouldn't have made a cent at our garage sale if some guy, driving by, hadn't noticed our lawn mower over to the side where we'd put it to get it out of the way, and stopped his car to look it over.

"How much you asking for it?" he asked, pulling the starter cord.

"It's not for sale," Mary answered, not looking up from painting her nails and adding "jerk" under her breath.

The guy didn't hear her because on his second pull the motor roared to life and by the time he'd tinkered with it a while, Mom was beside him saying, "Fifty dollars. As is."

"Thirty-five," the guy said.

"Forty-five."

"Forty."

"Forty-five."

The guy pulled out his wallet, counted out forty-five dollars, gave them to Mom and without another word turned and wheeled the mower to his car and slung it in the trunk.

"How'm I supposed to get lawn jobs this summer?" I asked, watching him drive away.

"We'll worry about that when summer gets here," Mom answered, gleefully putting the money in the tin box she'd set out to collect the river of cash she'd expected to come flooding in.

"I'd like to close this garage sale down right now," Mary said for the hundredth time. "We haven't sold a thing and it's embarrassing sitting out here with all this junk. What if some of my friends drive by?"

"Oh, I wish they would," Mom said, looking at our collection of old clothes, old books, discarded pictures and ornaments, parts of bikes, old patterns, old records, mismatched china, chipped clay pots and so on. "Maybe they'd buy something."

Mary snorted. "Would you buy any of this junk from them?"

"I might. Some of this stuff is probably collector's items. All we need is one good collector."

It went that way with everything she tried. She took a car load of books, mostly paperbacks, to the second hand book store figuring she was good for at least twenty bucks and came back with four, even. "They only gave me a nickel a-piece," she said sourly, "and I'm sure some of them were first editions."

"They were junk," Mary said. "Falling apart and half of them filled with crayon marks from when I was a kid and scribbled on everything. You were lucky they didn't charge you to throw them away."

"Maybe we could do some baby-sitting?" Mom suggested brightly, looking at us sideways.

"We?" Mary said, also looking sideways.

"Well, no. Not you. Me. What about all those little kids you used to sit for?"

"They grew up, Mom. Just like me. They've gone away to college."

"I don't know what's with kids nowadays," Mom sighed. "Just when you need them, they grow up and go away. Well, what else can we do? We still need a few more hundred."

"You sound like that old worrier that used to live here," Mary scowled. "The one that wouldn't let us run the air and fed us tuna casseroles. If you ask me, your imagination hit a road block several hundred dollars ago."

"My imagination's doing just fine..." Mom began, breaking off to take the mail from the mailman just pulling up to our mailbox.

"Oh, God!" she began, sounding panic-struck, "Here's something from the IRS. Now what? I filed on time, I know I did. Wait a minute! Do you suppose it could be...?" And while she's ripping at the seal she's saying, "No... couldn't be. It's only April. It's not possible. They never send out refunds this early. Well, what?" And then she's got the envelope open, is squinting at its contents and suddenly she's laughing like a lunatic. "You're not going to believe this," she said to Mary and me. "Not in a million years. Come and look for yourselves. It's for five hundred seventy-six dollars and twelve cents! Do you believe it? They've never paid me early before. Never. It's always been July. My thoughts did it! Just imagine! I've got my money!" She turned to Mary. "And you said it was impossible!"

"You're what's impossible," Mary glowered, gathering up her nail file and polish and heading for the house. "You filed your return early and they paid up. Period. No one in their right mind would believe imagination had anything to do with that. How can you possibly think it did?"

"Hold on a minute, Mary. Let's give a little credit where credit's due. Don't you see what I've accomplished? I set out just a few short weeks ago..."

"Make that a good six months..." Mary interrupted.

"To get together a thousand dollars," Mom continued, "Me, who's never had so much as a spare dime since the divorce. And I've done it. With twelve cents to spare, if you please. Now that may not seem much to you but to me it's little short of miraculous and I..."

"You're right," Mary said, softening just a little. "One thousand dollars is a nice tidy little sum for someone in your situation and I'm proud of you. Now, let it go. The car part, I mean, and go out and buy something really nice. Something luxurious. A terrific outfit to wear to Steve's graduation, maybe. You deserve it."

"I wouldn't dream of it, Mary," Mom said, waving the check and the cashbox. "First thing Monday morning this money's going in the bank. And I was right about it making me feel different. I feel terrific! Confident. Like a person who can *make* things happen."

Thirteen

She's someone who can make things happen all right, our Mom. She proved that to us again just a few days after she got her money stashed in the bank. Only this time we saw how making things happen can really go against you and in a heartbeat turn everything you've been working towards into a shambles and dreams into nightmares. It got that money out of the bank pretty darn quick, too, I tell you what...

What came next, at least to Mary's and my way of thinking, was an accident. And accidents being what they are – like, unexpected - we didn't know it was coming and so, for a few days anyway, Mom got to glory in her first "happening". She oozed confidence, laughed a lot and naturally, her talk of glories to come was non-stop.

Taking my cue from her and using the same upbeat tone, I said, "So now we get to go on to the good stuff, huh? Gonna go downtown get us a Beemer any day now, right?"

"Right," she said. "Any day now."

"Remind me again," I went on in the same breezy, upbeat way, "how it is we're going to get this car. I mean," I faltered in my act just a little, "what with getting the thousand together and all, I... I've kind've forgotten how it was you said it was going to happen."

"I never did say," she said, looking me straight in the eye, "because I don't know myself. But when the time comes, I'll know."

"But, like... Just what is it that's going to... uh... like, tip you off?"

"Oh... Well, for sure it'll come from within. It'll be a gut feeling kind of thing. Like a hunch. An intuition to go there... Be here... Do this... Stay away from the other... Or, could be I'll see a headline in the newspaper. Hear something in the words of a song. Or maybe it'll come in a dream. It'll be like a command! And I'll listen and I'll just do it. I'll *know*."

Eyes closed, smiling, she went on enumerating other possibilities but I was suddenly so overwhelmed with pity for her my eyes stung and I tuned her out because in my head I was seeing her – us – at Steve's graduation and I knew there would be no bright, shiny new car sitting outside for him and I cringed at how she'd feel about that. How she'd be able to look Mary and me in the face. How she'd ever explain it, get over it. I got up and left the room, sorry - I mean, *really sorry* - I'd asked.

The blow fell on a Friday night. At least it fell for Mom that afternoon but we didn't hear about it till she got home that night.

She came in quietly. So quietly that if I hadn't heard her car moments earlier I wouldn't have been expecting her at all. But suddenly she was standing in the doorway, looking so pale, so just plain defeated, you wondered what it was that was keeping her upright. And all of a sudden I felt like time was spinning backwards and the Mom of six years ago was standing there, her face showing the battle going on inside. The battle that was pitting the first thirty-eight years of her life against the fragile new beliefs of the past few years. The only difference was that the Mom of today was splattered, pretty near head to toe, with some kind of dark, messy gunk.

Mary, caught midway between stove and sink, a steaming saucepan in her hand, froze that way. "Mo-ther..." she breathed, suddenly as pale as Mom. "What is it?"

"It's..." Mom began while she's groping her way to a stool at the counter.

Right away, she's got me and Mary either side of her, both asking questions, both patting her back, both telling her that whatever it was, it was gonna be OK. Yet both of us wondering, I could tell from Mary's face and the sick feeling in my own stomach, if anything was ever going to be OK again.

"Go get some paper towels, Jeff," Mary ordered and I did, not even stopping to ask why she didn't go get them herself.

When I got back, Mary had Mom installed in an armchair and was gingerly pulling off her splattered shoes using just thumbs and forefingers, her face saying "gross" for her. And then she was studying Mom thoughtfully, figuring, I could tell, what approach to use to get Mom to pull herself together and tell us what was going on.

I saw, from the way her face was arranging itself into a fierce scowl, that she'd decided on the tough approach. Why not? It's what she's best at. And then she's growling, "Time to turn it off now, Mom. We're fresh out of sympathetic words. At least, until we know what happened. So tell us, did you kill somebody?"

Mom shook her head.

"Is Steve OK?"

Mom nodded.

"Did you get in a wreck?"

Mom shook her head.

"Do you have an incurable disease you just found out about?"

Mom shook her head.

"The bank's kicking us out because you didn't pay the mortgage?"

Again Mom shook her head. And with each nod or shake of her head I could see Mary relaxing, could feel the knots in my own stomach loosening.

"As far as I'm concerned," Mary said, straightening, "that about covers it. If it's none of the above, it's sure not worth crying over. You're covered head to toe in some kind of smelly gunk but, hey, so what? No big deal." And she got up, went back into the kitchen, picked the pan up off the stove and dumped it's contents into a strainer in the sink as though Mom's bizarre appearance was something that happened every day.

"I did something so awful... So unbelievable... So horrendous... I got fired." Mom whimpered from her armchair.

"You got fired?" Mary yelped, letting go of her pots and pans with a crash and whirling to face Mom. "You mean the old hemorrhoid let you go?" She burst into crazed laughter. "That's not something to be upset about, Mom. That's the best news I've heard all year. Harry doesn't have a business without you. You *are* his business. You're the one with the taste. The nifty ideas. Quick! Tell us what you did. I hope it's something really, really bad!" She paused, her eyes narrowing. "Something terrible beyond belief. Something he's deserved since the day you walked in his door and turned his trashy little business into SOMETHING!"

She got herself back in front of Mom, "OK, now begin at the beginning and don't leave out a single thing. Especially the part where you hauled off and told him where to go and where to shove it."

"I... I dropped a can of paint," Mom began.

"I could have told you that," Mary said, but looking interested in spite of herself. "So you dropped a can of paint." She brightened. "You dropped it on Harry?"

Mom shook her head. "I was over at the Alderson's..." she began, her face muffled by a wad of tissues so we really had to strain to hear what she was saying. "They're those darling..."

"We know, we know," Mary interrupted. "They've been part of our dinner-time conversations for the last six months. They're those darling gazillionaires from up north who are moving down here."

"Tomorrow!" Mom wailed. "They're due in tomorrow with all their kids and all their grandkids and I don't know how many house guests and I was over at their place for a fi... final inspection and..." her voice trailed off, her face went blank, then all horror-struck again.

"I like what I'm hearing so for," Mary encouraged. "It's a good plot. The Aldersons are due in tomorrow. You were over there. You dropped a can of paint. Now give us the punch line. Where did you drop it?"

Mom took a deep breath. "The house is – was - so beautiful. Just spectacular. Every detail in place. All the beds made up. Bath linens in place. Fresh flowers everywhere. Fridge stocked. Logs in all the fireplaces. A dream home..."

"Never mind all the fluff," Mary interrupted. "All your houses are dream homes. It's the paint we're interested in right now. We want all the gory details."

"I was in the kitchen and I saw that Clyde... He's..."

"We know! We know! Clyde's the painter," Mary interrupted again. "The Michael Angelo of faux."

"Right. Well I saw he'd left all his acrylics and stains and varnishes on the island in the kitchen. I mean, really! What was he thinking about? He'd just gone off and left everything. Brushes. Turpentine. Drop cloths."

"He was going to come back for final touch-ups?" I suggested.

"That's what I thought," Mom said. "But I checked all the places I'd told him about and it was all done. It looked beautiful. The man really does have a gift."

"I'm getting the picture," Mary said. "Clyde left his paints. You picked them up. And you dropped one of them...

all of them?" She leaned forward, lowering her voice. "Tell us, Mom, where? Where did you drop the paint?"

"In the entry hall," Mom said, so fast all the words ran together.

"Wow!" Mary gasped. "The entry hall! Way to go, Momma. I mean, if you're going to drop paint, that's the place to let if fly! Must've gone every which way, huh? What color was it?"

"It was a mahogany stain. A full gallon." Mom moaned. "And Mary, please drop this act of yours. I know you're trying to see me through a crisis but this is one occasion where no attitude you can adopt is going to make me feel better. It's too awful. I've never seen a worse mess in my life. Never. Not even when you were a toddler and finger painted the living room upholstery. I... It just all happened so fast! I was hurrying to the front door with it. I was going to take it all back to the office because I knew Clyde would need it and wouldn't be able to get back in. I mean, how could he? I had the key. And I don't know... I must have tripped or slipped or something. Next thing I know the can's just exploding off the floor. Up the walls. All over the tile entry hall. Do you remember how much trouble we had getting that grout just right? It got the carpeting everywhere. The stairs. The living room. The dining room. It looked just like a bomb went off. I didn't know what to do. Where to begin. I couldn't take a step without leaving tracks. And then... Harry walked in."

"Oh, my," Mary gloated. "I bet that fake, sunshiny smile of his came off in a big hurry, huh!"

"He went crazy," Mom said. "Berserk! And you can't blame the man. Anybody would have. I know I would. Only... I didn't have anyone to blame," her head drooped. "Just myself."

"I don't see the problem," Mary said, right in character. "I consider it divine justice that Harry's got a real mess on his hands this time - not just one of his spiteful little hissy fits - and since he fired you, he's going to have to deal with it all by himself. I hope the Aldersons let him have it big time."

"If only life was as simple as you'd like to make it, Mary," Mom sighed. "But there is such a thing as taking responsibility for your own actions. Regardless of what you think of Harry, or me, I'm responsible for that... That catastrophe."

"Fine. Go ahead and take it. Beat yourself over the head. What good is it going to do? If you're fired, you're fired. You're out of it."

"There's a lot I can do," Mom said, seeming to come out of her fog long enough to remember she was the kind of person who could make things happen. "And it's got nothing to do with Harry. The Aldersons are charming people – even if they weren't, it wouldn't make a difference – nobody should have to walk into a mess like that. Think how you would feel if it was you bringing your family to your ultimate dream home. I've got Clyde over there right now working on the walls. Thank God I was able to reach him. But it's the carpeting. The tiles. That grout. It's all got to be replaced. And I can't get hold of any of those floor people. They've got an answering machine on at the office. Nobody's answering the home phones. Nobody's answering the cell phones. I've just got to track them down. I mean, they can't have just up and vaporized, can they?"

"Happens all the time on Aliens," I said.

"Stay out of it, Mom," Mary urged. "You're the one always preaching about how good comes out of adversity. Well, here's your big chance. You can go out on your own now and..." her face brightened. "Think! You've got the money to do it now. Your thousand dollars! Oh, Mom! Imagine! You can start your own company. All of Harry's clients are really yours. They love you! They'll give you referrals!"

"I'm afraid not, Mary," Mom said. "I... Well, somebody's got to pay for that mess I made. It's clearly my responsibility. I dropped the paint. Harry said..."

"Harry said!" Mary repeated, her eyes glinting. "What do you mean, Harry said? Harry's out of the loop now, Mom. He fired you, remember?"

"Don't yell at me, Mary," Mom said, getting to her feet and heading for the phone, all business. "I created havoc. I don't intend to give Harry the added satisfaction of pointing me out as the reason his business failed. I couldn't live with myself knowing I hadn't done everything in my power to set things straight. Unfortunately, one thousand dollars isn't going to come close to covering the damage, but... it's a start."

"Mom!" Mary exploded. "I... We... We're not going to let you use that money to get Harry off the hook. It's yours. You went through hell to get it. Besides, isn't that what insurance is all about? To cover sh... uh, stuff like that?"

"He says he doesn't have any," Mom said wearily, dialing a number. "But even if he did, I feel morally responsible. Anyway, it's too late to argue. I've already taken the money out of the bank."

If Mary was mad before, she turned into a raging bonfire then telling Mom that the Alderson's insurance would cover it. If not them, then Clyde's. Or the floor people's. Mom didn't even bother to answer. Just kept dialing that number.

"Do you remember who you're trying to call?" I asked after Mary had finally flounced off to some party she was supposed to have been at hours earlier and Mom was still dialing.

"The floor people. Who else?" she said wearily. "Where can they be? I mean, this is a business we're talking here. They must have some kind of emergency numbers. What if their warehouse went up in flames?"

Personally, I thought I'd be more worried about handing over my thousand bucks and having to go find another job, than the floor people. "What good's it going to do if you do track them down?" I asked. "They won't go rip out carpet and tear up tile tonight, will they?"

"I guess not," Mom said, reluctantly hanging up the phone. "It is after eight. I'll try again first thing in the morning. If I can just get hold of them early enough there's a chance they could have it all fixed up before the Alderson's get in tomorrow. You'd be surprised how fast they work. And maybe Mary's right. Maybe someone - the Aldersons - perhaps, will have some kind of home-owner's policy to cover the damage."

"Tomorrow's Saturday," I reminded her. "They don't work Saturdays, do they?"

"They might for a thousand dollar bonus," Mom said, with just the trace of a smile. "They say money talks, Jeff. For the first time in my life I'm going to be able to put that to the test. That gives me a good feeling even though," and the smile faded, "it's not the way I'd have chosen to spend it."

I could see, now she was through trying to phone for the night, that all the other trouble she was in was starting to crowd in on her and I couldn't think of a thing to say that would make any of it go away. Mary'd said it all. I thought I'd best just leave her to it.

"You know what upsets me the most?" she said as I headed for my room.

I waited for her to go on.

"It's what in the world I could have been thinking to make all that happen? What was going on in my head?"

"You probably weren't thinking at all," I said. "Just hurrying through a house with an armload of paint is all."

"No, no. The thought always comes first. There's no such thing as an accident. I guess I must have been thinking angry, destructive thoughts to have made all that happen."

"Harry?" I suggested. "The Aldersons? Michael Angelo?"

"Maybe," Mom said. "Maybe all of them, one way or another. The Aldersons did move up their arrival date. Harry forever belittling, downplaying, everything I ever do, taking credit for all of it himself. Never ever sticking up for me when clients get exactly what they order and then don't like it. Clyde going off leaving a mess like that so I had to go back to the office when I had errands of my own to run. Lots of them. Had to get to the bank," she made a face. "I was going to make a deposit. Never thought I'd be emptying my account."

"Come on, Mom," I said. "Stop trying to make yourself out a villain. With all you had going on, hurrying and all, no wonder you dropped the paint."

"Maybe I didn't drop it," she faltered. "Maybe I threw it?"

"That's one you'll have to figure out for yourself," I said. "Personally, I'd say what Mary always says and I'm sorry to cuss but, Hey! Once in a while, shit happens!"

Fourteen

I woke up the next morning feeling kind've depressed wondering how in the world Mary and I were going to get Mom through the next couple days.

Dragging, I headed for the kitchen expecting to see them arguing again but when I got out there they looked just like they always did: Mary with electric curlers sticking out all over her head and a piece of dry toast in front of her, Mom reading the paper and drinking coffee. She gave me an absent-minded pat on the head when I sat down and began pouring my cereal.

"So..." I began after I'd downed the first few mouthfuls. "You tracked down those floor goons yet?"

She nodded without looking up from the paper and I saw she wasn't reading it at all, was just staring at it blank-eyed which meant her mind was racing behind the stare.

It really bugs me how sometimes she can rattle on so fast about stuff it's hard to figure where she's coming from. And other times it's like she needs a jump start to get word one out of her.

As though she'd reached some kind of decision, she suddenly straightened, set the paper aside, cleared her throat, and began, "I got the guy's wife on the phone. Al, the floor guy, I mean. He's out running errands right now. He doesn't have his beeper on him. Never does on Saturdays, she said. And when he's done his errands, he's headed straight for the track. Another thing he always does Saturdays during racing season, she said. She doesn't expect him till late tonight, but she will give him my message."

For a moment she drooped, then straightened quickly and beamed a tentative kind of smile in my direction. "I've been thinking and the way I see it there's only one thing left to do and that's just go to the track and find him," she said. "Want to come? It'll be fun. You know how I've always loved horses. Maybe you will, too. You could watch the races while I hunt down Al and bribe him to go fix up the Alderson place."

While she's talking, Mary's ten terrible nails are drumming the counter with such fury I'm surprised they don't all come flying off the way they do sometimes when she's rough on them. Next, she let's out this long sigh like it's the last day of intelligent life on the planet and says, "I wish Steve was here to talk to you. I've tried and tried and nothing I say gets through to you and now you're going to take your life savings and waste a whole day trying to force them on some jerk who'll be impossible to find anyway. Who'll probably laugh in your face if you do – find him, I mean - when none of it's any of your damn business anymore. Can't you get that through your head, Mom? Harry fired you. You're out of a job. You're going to need that money to keep going while you regroup."

"Everything you said just might be true, Mary, except the part about it being impossible to find Al. You know how I hate that word. Nothing's impossible. I just have to know I did everything in my power to correct that hideous mess I made. I want to go forward with a clear conscience and good references. If not from Harry, then at least from the Aldersons. Besides, neither Jeff nor I have ever been to the races. It's a gorgeous day and don't forget, you get what you think about. I've already imagined myself finding Al and him being only too happy to run over and replace the damaged carpet – there was a ton of it left over – and the grout. And Monday morning…"

"We'll all live happily ever after," Mary sneered.

"Don't be so angry, honey," Mom pleaded. "This is an attempt on my part to correct the damage I've done by spending a few hundred dollars that are mine to do with as I please and then move on fearlessly to become the kind of woman you've always wanted me to be."

"You're an impossible woman," Mary stormed and began yanking the curlers out of her hair with such force I couldn't tell if the tears in her eyes were from rage or pain.

"You're coming with us?" I asked, hoping she wasn't.

"I don't have a choice do I? I'm not about to let you two out on your own. It'd be a case of the blind leading the blind. You know Mom won't be able to find her glasses and will go stumbling around, blind as a bat, looking for one face out of thousands. You know you'll take off the minute you get there like you always do and Mom'll spend the whole entire day looking for you instead of him. I bet Mom doesn't even know where the track is."

"I suppose you do." I said.

"Of course, I do," she said, getting her very efficient look. "I looked it up on the map as soon as I heard Mom on the phone with Al's wife earlier." She couldn't help but smirk at the surprised look on our faces. "You didn't really think I'd let you two go off without me, did you? Even though I think the chances of finding the guy are less than one in a million and him agreeing to leave and go patch up those floors one in a zillion, I'm going with you. And don't either one of you forget for one second that I'm the one who hates family outings more than all the other things I hate put together."

She tried to glare at us again but couldn't pull it off. "I also called the track because I knew Mom wouldn't think to do that either. The gates open at twelve. We need to leave by eleven at the latest. We'll take my car. Be ready." Tossing her head like the whole day was her idea from the first, she stalked out of the room.

When we heard the bathroom door crash shut behind her, Mom said, "I'm so glad she wants to come with us."

"I'm not," I groaned. "She'll wreck everything. She'll be bossing us around all day long."

"It's not so much that she's bossy," Mom said. "It's that she's very, very protective. She loves us. Anyway, once we get there she'll be on unfamiliar territory just like us. That'll subdue her for a while, make her forget her mothering role. And when we give Al the money, get that house back to normal, the Aldersons thrilled, Harry off my back forever, she'll see things my way and be glad we took the high road. And don't forget, she loves to drive and I hate it. Be glad for that, if nothing else."

Even with Mary driving, which meant we got there twice as fast as Mom would have and didn't get lost, that was the longest drive I've ever been on. It seemed like we drove forever and when we did get near the place, the traffic slowed to a crawl and we were having our typical Florida day which meant we were all hot as hell and I was starting to feel sick. By the time we parked the car Mary had lost a finger nail and was raging because the humidity in the air had taken all the curl out of her hair.

Mom told her she looked beautiful anyway and that only made her madder.

Even though we were early, there was a mob of people ahead of us waiting to get through the gate and I started worrying in case the first race started before I got a chance to figure how it all worked. Like me, everyone had thought to bring binoculars but they were all talking a mile a minute about horses - thoroughbreds they called them - and hot tips and how such and such a horse in such and such a race was a sure winner, and about blood lines and I wondered if all that was making Mom and Mary feel as ignorant as it was me. But when I looked I saw Mary's thoughts were far away and Mom was already hard at work scanning faces and could have been in the checkout line at the supermarket for all the interest she had in what was going on around her.

Finally we got close enough to see, actually see, the entrance gate and then down to about six people in front of us and then one of two men who were standing nearby talking, came forward and tapped Mom on the shoulder.

"You planning on taking the boy in with you, ma'am?" he asked, nodding at me.

"Yes, I am," she said, looking from one to the other with a big question mark on her face.

"They don't allow kids," the other guy said, and I felt like I'd been punched in the stomach.

"How old do they have to be?" Mom faltered.

"Eighteen. State law."

Mom's face went from blank to stunned to nothing to smiling. "Isn't that lucky," she beamed, putting her arm around my shoulder. "Jeff just turned eighteen last week."

Both men stared hard at me and I frowned back trying to make my face look eighteen. I wished I'd at least worn jeans instead of cut-offs, and I quick folded my arms over my *Motley Crue* T-shirt, thinking of all the serious ones stacked, unworn, in my closet at home.

"Sure could have fooled me," the second man said.

"Both of my sons are built small," Mom babbled. "My eldest son is twenty-two and he's only an inch or two taller than Jeff."

I was awfully happy Steve wasn't there for them to see his six feet plus inches.

We were at the gate then and Mom said, "Three, please."

"How old is the boy?" the woman in the ticket booth asked.

"Eighteen," Mom, Mary and I said together.

"Don't look like no eighteen to me," the woman said suspiciously. "You got some ID?"

"Lord, Almighty," Mom snapped. "Of course not. Just because a boy looks young for his age, doesn't mean we have to carry a birth certificate around with us, does it?"

"I got to see some identification," the woman insisted.

"Show her your driver's license, Jeff," Mary said giving me a mean jab with her elbow, and saying Jeff so it sounded like jerk, but yet smiling at the lady all the while. "He looks just like Steve in it," she went on conversationally, as though the woman had known Steve since birth. "Cute. Wait till you see."

"You know perfectly well he doesn't..." Mom began, and then stopped and smiled. "Yes, Jeff, show her your driver's license. That should do it."

Sweating, I groped in my short's pocket wondering how in hell I was supposed to pull out a license I didn't have.

"Oh, my God," Mary sighed. "Don't tell me you forgot it!" She turned to the lady. "Three times he flunks the test and when he finally nails it he leaves it home." She turned back to me, "What were you planning on doing? Framing it?"

"The boy is eighteen, Mildred," the man who had first spoken to us said to the impatient woman. "I was at the shindig they threw for him last week myself."

"Oh, Mr. Winfield, sir," the woman gasped, looking real flustered. "Excuse me! I didn't take note of you standing there. I mean, I'd never expect to see you this side of gate." Simpering, she handed the three tickets to Mom without a second glance and focused all her attention on Mr. Winfield and the guy with him, whoever they were.

"What a hunk," Mary said, as we hurried away.

"What's that, honey?" Mom asked

"I said that guy was a hunk. That Mr. Winfield." Mary said. "And a sweetheart too. Must be pretty important the way that woman over-reacted. Just your age too, Mom. Don't you notice anything?"

I didn't think Mom had even looked at the guy so I was really surprised when she said, "Yes to all of the above. And I believe he's quite well known. I know I've seen his picture somewhere. We should have stayed to thank him but I was terrified that woman would get back to Jeff's ID if we did."

"You're such a jerk, Jeff," Mary said, forgetting the men and remembering the trouble at the gate. "You nearly blew the whole day. All that fuss last Christmas to get you a wallet and you don't even carry it on you."

"You're the jerk," I yelled at her. "Wouldn't matter if I had twenty wallets, would it, if I don't have a driver's license to put in any one of them and no money either. Why would I carry a wallet?"

"Because you're supposed to, fool. If those men hadn't lied for you we'd be on our way home now. At least if you'd pulled out a wallet you'd have looked more like an a-dult."

"Is a-dult," I imitated her pronunciation, "a whole new look you get when you carry a wallet around? Excuse me, I didn't know."

"A-dults," Mary went on, ignoring my question, "can be counted on to forget either their license or their money or their credit cards, but they do not forget their wallets. You looked just like a dumb school boy."

"He is a school boy, Mary," Mom said sharply. "And stop fussing. We're in. That's all that matters. I wonder where I should start my search?"

We were walking between rows of seats. Some out in the open, going in rows almost down to the track itself. Others, under cover, rising in banks like a stadium. Right away I knew I wanted to be either right up by the track or else up in the top row, under the roof.

"Soon's you find Al, give him the money," I told Mom, pointing, "that's where you should go sit. Right up there at the top where you can see everything. You know, watch all those horses you love so much! And I'll just go down there by the track, right there in the middle, where I guess the races finish? That way, if you need me, all you have to do is wave."

"Maybe we're not allowed to go up there," Mom said, thinking out loud. "Maybe they're reserved or something?"

"Let's sit in them anyway," Mary said, "see if anyone tells us to move. We look dorky standing around here like a bunch of yahoos."

"We should get a program first," Mom said. "Try to figure this whole thing out. Like when it begins and when it ends? Do they have an intermission? Then Jeff can go have a look around. Check out the horses... Whatever..."

"Hey, you're the one who loves horses," I reminded her. "Don't you want to come with me see them first? Maybe you could pick a winner."

"No, honey, not now. First things first. After I find Al, maybe. Just for a minute. But not to pick a winner. Good Lord! You know how I feel about gambling. It's insanity. A fool's game."

"This whole day's a fool's game, if you ask me," Mary grumbled.

"Just go buy a program, Jeff," Mom said digging in her purse and handing me a ten. "No, better make it three. We'll have one each in case you two can't take being around me all day. And hurry back. We need to pick a rendezvous point where we can meet up every so often."

I took my sweet time getting the programs from this guy who told me he couldn't break a ten but to go ahead and take the programs and come back later for my change. Him, I understood and I hung around until I knew he'd sold enough to make change and then it took me a while to find Mom and Mary because the place was filling up and they weren't sitting at the top like I'd told them. They were sitting near where I left them, looking half-mad, half-worried. They didn't see me so I ducked away again and took some more time to go check out the track.

It swept away in a broad, tan-colored oval, looking smooth and ready, like it couldn't wait to get messed up, between twin white fences around the greenest grass I'd ever seen in my life.

Opposite the grandstand, on the far side of the track, was a whole bunch of boards with flashing lights and horses names and numbers and I thought I'd better ask someone what they all meant because it would take me all day to figure it out myself.

And all the time I was dawdling, looking for things to look at, if you know what I mean, I was trying to figure out why I didn't want to give Mom the programs. Then it came to me: I was afraid once she got it all figured out, she'd set off to find Al and once that was done, she'd drag us away to supervise the clean up at the Alderson's. God, no wonder I wasn't in a hurry. No way was I up for that.

Still, and without meaning to, I found myself heading back towards them.

"It took you long enough," Mary scowled.

"You can run along now, honey," Mom said, maybe seeing how I was dragging my feet. "This seems to be as good a place as any. Just check back in between races. As soon as I find Al, we'll be on our way."

She didn't have to tell me twice. I was out of there.

FIFTEEN

I headed off down the side steps of the grandstand, came around a corner and said "Wow!" out loud before I could stop myself. I mean, I knew the place was all about horses racing but the horses being walked around in this little circle place right in front of me weren't like any horses I'd ever seen before. Although, just thinking that, makes me realize the only other horses I'd seen up till then were in cowboy movies on TV and the horses in front of me that day looked like gods compared to them.

It was like they were horses, all right, I mean, you wouldn't think they were some other species, but they were, like, more than horses, too. Like aristocrats, I thought, and I could see why they were called thoroughbreds. Standing there watching them being groomed and sponged, pampered and saddled, seeing their beautiful heads held high and aloof, their large, dark eyes ignoring the little groups of people fussing around each of them and focusing instead on some inner scene not visible to us poor humans, I thought they were the most awesome creatures I'd ever seen.

One minute I'd be looking at all that smooth, stationary, shining sleekness set up on those thin, fine legs and thinking how fragile they looked, next minute, my eyes would take in one being walked around the paddock and I could see the underlay of muscle moving smooth and easy underneath all that gloss, and I'd think I never saw so much power waiting to let loose in my life.

I've seen people with their envious friends fussing over incredible sports cars the way those horses were being fussed over, but that was different. Cars don't live or breathe and I thought it seemed like an insult almost to put saddles and men on those horses' backs and make them run around a stupid track like they were a bunch of jocks. In fact, I thought they made all us people standing around gawking at them look ugly by comparison and I was sure that if they were free to do what they wanted, they would have better things to do than stand around waiting to see which one of us could run the fastest.

Some of them, their bodies covered in loose fitting blankets, were being led around the enclosure by kids who didn't look any older than me. There were even some girls! I mean, think about owning a horse like one of those and then letting a girl lead it around!

I remember I suddenly saw a picture in my mind of our house and the street we live on and it all seemed so little and cramped and just plain boring when I thought of the openness and space those horses must have come from. And I thought of me going off to school every day and Mom driving her wreck to deal with a boss she hated and Steve busting his gut over some dumb diploma so he could get a job in an office and none of it seemed right to me. It made me feel like the human race must've taken a wrong turn somewhere.

I wished I could trade places with any one of those kids leading the horses around. Especially the girls. Man, I would walk so proud if someone trusted me with one of them.

The easy, relaxed feel of the enclosure changed when the jockeys came out. Little, bitty guys they were, dressed in britches and boots and "silks" which are the brightest colored shirts you'll ever see on a grown man. They had helmets on their heads with goggles set up above the peak and they each carried a saddle. More than the bystanders, I thought, the horses sensed their arrival, their long easy strides picking up from a Sunday afternoon kind of stroll to a livelier pace, their heads going even higher, ears pricking forward, eyes losing the distant, far away look and zeroing in on now. Their muscles tightened up like they were pulling themselves together, not wanting, maybe, to have saddles and bridles put on them? But hey, maybe they loved it? Couldn't wait to get on the track? How would I know? But I could see the more stuff that was done to them, the more they fidgeted and swung away from the grooms holding them until in the end they were downright nervous and some of them broke a sweat that lathered white under the reins on their necks.

When the jockeys were finally mounted, the horses looked bigger and the men smaller, and I wondered what it could possibly be like to be a jockey, so small, sitting up there on top of all that power moving and surging beneath you. Scary, I thought. Real scary. Or maybe not?

A loudspeaker blared then. Something about the first race, and the horses and riders fell into a line of sorts that made its way out of the enclosure and towards the track and the crowd of people surged forward for a last look and then they, too, hurried away to watch the race. But I followed the horses as best I could from my side of the rail and saw the grooms leading them into a terrible looking contraption that the loudspeaker told me was the starting gate. A few of the horses thought it was a terrible looking thing, too, and made a huge fuss about getting in it and one of them nearly threw his jockey before they put a blindfold on and him and got him safely inside.

I couldn't imagine what it could be like for either a horse or a jockey to be shut in there with no room to move, waiting for it to go up or open, whatever it was going to do. Even just watching, my heart was pounding and my hands were sweaty and then, Wham! The gate flew open, the horses were out, and I heard what sounded like thunder, the pounding of their hooves, and saw bits of earth flying and I got a glimpse of hugely muscled, straining animals and the flash of the jockeys colors and then the crowd surged forward, screaming, and I couldn't see a thing.

I took off running alongside the track looking for an opening where I could see the race, but by the time I saw a likely looking space and crawled on my hands and knees through the crowd at the fence, the horses were already on the other side of the track and moving... God, so fast! But push and shove as I might, I really couldn't see which one was in the lead. I looked pleadingly at a very big woman who was screaming a horse's name and she noticed me.

"Let the kid in," she yelled, nudging the guy next to her.

"What's that?" he roared, mad at being distracted. And then he saw me. "Beat it," he yelled even louder. "Kids ain't got no right being here." And he went back to yelling at the horses and I wriggled out of there and went pounding alongside the track again and I knew, because I heard the thunder of hooves approaching, that the horses were right there, so I threw myself on the ground and saw their legs stream by. Three or four together, then a couple more and then another, all by itself.

"How many times do they go around the track?" I yelled to the first person, a guy, I saw when I was upright again.

"Once," his lips read, and he held up a finger.

Damn! The whole race was going to be over and I wouldn't get to see any of it the way I was going and I started running again. Just then I saw a bunch of people ahead of me leave the rails and I dived in like I was stealing a base and got myself right up against the rail before the crowd closed in behind me and wow! What a view! I figured I was about twenty feet in front of the finish line - if the finish line was what I thought it was - and this time there were two horses way out in front, then a bunch of them in a huddle like they were running a race of their own, then a couple of stragglers, all of them stretched out flat, like, close to the ground, and looking nothing at all like they had in the paddock. Suddenly I remembered the binoculars swinging from my neck, and I brought them up and focused and Lord, what a sight! Those horses were fighters! You could see it in the way they strained, necks out, tails streaming, giving everything they had, giving beyond what they had... concentrating. And those little bitty jockeys seemed like a part of them, spread out along their necks like bits of colored paper, urging them on, one arm of each flailing a whip, though why they would want a whip when every horse out there was busting his gut, I wouldn't know. And then they were coming around the bend and I dropped my binoculars as they loomed larger and larger down the track towards me.

Again I heard the approaching thunder of their hooves, their heavy breathing, the shouts of the jockeys urging them to go faster yet and then they were past me and the crowd which had been going crazy while they were coming up the track exploded in a roar and the race was over.

I didn't know for sure which horse had won. I knew there were three of them right there close together but which one made it, I didn't know. It had all happened too fast for me and anyway I didn't care. All I knew was, I loved it. That this was the best way to spend a day I'd ever come across. Better than football or baseball or water skiing or anything else, because this had the horses.

I was half way back to the enclosure to see what happened next when I remembered Mom and Mary. To myself I said, Shit, did an about face and started off in their direction. Had she found Al? Would she be getting ready to leave? Felt to me while I ran that I'd been away a lot longer than the time it took to run a race. Felt more like I'd been gone a month or so and that my whole life had changed direction in that time. Going back to them brought back all the reasons why we'd come in the first place and as I remembered, I slowed to a walk. It was all so dumb I felt like I didn't want any part of it. Two ding-dongs hanging around the stands, one of them thinking she was going to find one face in this mess of people, the other yawning with boredom and worrying about a broken finger nail and wishing she could go home. I didn't want to see them. I wanted to be back around the horses. Damn. But there they were and they'd seen me and were waving.

"Did you find him?" I asked.

Mom shook her head, frowning. "Not yet," she said.

"We're not going to either," Mary said, all pouty. "We might as well be looking for a needle in a haystack. There's got to be a million people here. What a waste of a day."

"Well, there's no hurry, is there?" I said, wanting them to calm down, relax, take their time. "There's still nine more races to go. Plenty of time."

"There's a very big hurry," Mom said sharply. "The sooner I find Al, the sooner I get the Alderson house behind me. Lord, I feel like I've got a millstone around my neck."

"What if you find him and he doesn't want to leave?" I asked. "I mean, people come here to bet, don't they? What if he's on a roll?"

Mom's mouth turned down in a sneer. "If he's gambling, he's more likely to be losing. Big time," she said. "Gambling's a loser's game, Jeff. Everybody knows that. I expect by the time I find him, he'll be only too happy to take my thousand and leave."

"Well, if he comes every Saturday, there's got to be a reason. Maybe he's one of the lucky ones."

"There's no such thing as luck," Mom snapped. "I thought I'd made that clear. You get what you think about."

"Maybe," Mary began, and there was a wicked gleam in her eye. "Maybe he thinks about winning mega bucks every single Friday night and bingo! He shows up here Saturdays to collect." She pulled a tiny pocket calculator out of her purse and began punching in numbers. "Look," she shaded the calculator with her other hand so we could see the numbers dancing, acid green, across the screen. "If he'd put fifty bucks on that horse, Dan's Deluge, in the last race which was running at twenty to one he'd..."

"What's twenty to one mean?" I interrupted.

"It means that someone around here – someone who knows about these things, thought... get that, Mom, thought - that that horse had only one chance in twenty of winning that race. But it went and beat the odds. So if he'd put fifty bucks on it, he'd have won," she waved the calculator, "one thousand dollars!"

"Jeez," I breathed. "One thousand dollars. It doesn't seem possible!"

"Nobody in their right mind would put fifty dollars on a horse race, Mary," Mom interrupted, sounding testy. "Certainly Al wouldn't. He's got a wife, a family, to support. He probably just likes horses. Like me. But you've given me an idea. Maybe if he does have a little fling here and there, five dollars or so on something he likes the look of, then the place for me to find him would be at those betting windows over there."

"You can always try," Mary said. "But there are betting windows all over this place. How're you going to know which ones he'll use?"

"Oh, if only you two knew what he looked like," Mom anguished. "It would make this all so much easier. I guess I'll just have to try them all."

"How come you know so much about all this?" I asked Mary after Mom left. "You been studying up?"

"I keep my eyes and ears open, dork. While Mom's scanning faces, I'm scanning that big board over there; listening to what people're saying. And Mom's wrong, I saw plenty of intelligent-looking people over there at the windows putting down some pretty big bucks."

"So what's the word on the next race, genius?" I asked.

"Don't know," she mumbled, scanning her program. "I heard something about a horse called Suzy's Delight, number seven, but then you showed up and I lost track of the whole thing."

"Want to come with me down to the enclosure?" I asked, amazing myself I'd want to do anything with her. "You could look them over for yourself."

"Why would I want to do that? I'm not throwing my money away on a stupid horse race. Besides, you can't tell which one is going to win by looking at them. If it was that easy there'd be no point in racing them. It would be a foregone conclusion."

"You can't tell by looking at a program either," I said. "It's not like they're dish towels in the Sears' catalog."

"Get lost, will you," she groaned.

"I am. I'm gonna go down take a look at Suzy's Delight," I said.

Back at the enclosure, they were busy saddling the horses for the next race but damned if I knew which one was number seven.

"How can you tell which horse is which?" I asked a guy wearing riding clothes who looked like he knew a lot about horses.

"Look for the numbers," he said. "On the horse's saddlecloths. Which horse you looking for?"

"Number seven."

He nodded. "Suzy's Delight. That's her right there. The bay."

The bay? Don't ask me. The horse he pointed to was the one nearest us and I was able to get a pretty good look at her although it would have helped if all the people around her would have stepped aside. She didn't fidget around as much as some of the others, especially when her jockey got on her and yet she seemed alert, holding her head up nice and high. "She sure looks fast," I said to the guy in riding clothes.

He gave a snort. "Looks don't tell it like it is, son. That horse has never won a race. You want fast you put your money on Number Four over there. That horse travels faster than light. Hasn't been beaten all season."

He pointed to a horse that was tearing up the place. Three guys were trying to hold him still so a young girl could get a saddle on him.

I didn't wait to hear anymore. Couldn't wait to get back to Mary and tell her what I'd heard. Tell her for all her know-it-all attitude she didn't know beans about nothing.

But when I got close to where I'd left her I saw Mom was back and from the way they were talking instead of arguing I thought maybe Mom had found the guy and was ready to leave so I beat it quick down to the paddock again.

The horses were already on their way to the gate when I got there so I made a beeline for as near the finish line as I could get to try and beat the crowds.

From where I waited I could see they were having a terrible time getting number four into the gate and the jockey looked like he was going to get thrown and trampled to death. I looked over at Suzy's Delight, hoping that that number four goon wasn't going to get her all upset but she looked as majestic as ever and even slightly bored. Then suddenly the gate was up and again the thunder of hooves made my own heart beat faster, as though I'd picked up adrenaline from them, and everyone around me was screaming for their horse. This time I was screaming too. Screaming my lungs out for Number Four, wanting, I guess, to prove Mary wrong.

He came out of the gate like a bat out of hell. So did most of the other horses. All except Suzy who came out like a fine old sail boat. Smooth, clean and last.

"Go for it Number Four," I goaded, "Move it!" and smiled seeing Mary's horse still running last. I couldn't see anything for a minute and then on the other side a blur of the jockey's colors and their helmets, seeming to skim along the top of the rail, and then gone again so I couldn't see them and then there was a surge as the crowd pressed forward and they were coming towards us, flat out.

I fumbled for my binoculars but couldn't get them focused in time and the whole field was streaming right by me and the very earth on which I stood seemed to shake and I could feel the urgency in the horses and the tension in the jockeys urging them on and I could smell the sweat that stained their necks and flanks and hear the creak of saddles and the labored breathing and then they were back around the turn and I felt shaken, as though there was an emergency and I ought to be running too. I remembered the binoculars and focused them in front of the horses. This time I was ready for them. I saw Number Four still up in front and then I saw Suzy had moved up, too, and wasn't running last anymore

"Go on, Four!" I yelled. "Go for it! You can do it!" And then they were rounding the next to last curve, all in a bunch with number four just a little ahead and then I saw a helmet coming up on the outside, fast, but I couldn't see its number. I leaned out as far as I could and saw them coming out of the last turn and heading straight for me and still I couldn't tell. A bay horse? Damn, they all looked bay to me and then the crowd was roaring down at the end by the enclosure, the sound moving along with the horses.

I kept on yelling, too, even knowing my voice was lost in the general roar. But then I stopped and listened instead, really listened, to what everyone was yelling and it was Suzy's Delight! Every voice there hollering for that one horse...

"Lord, Lord! Will you look at that animal move," someone behind me said though I didn't look to see who. Then three horses were coming up to the finish, faster and faster yet, and the outside horse was passing. Had passed. Had won.

"She did it!" I said to no one in particular. "She did it!" And darned if I know if I was talking about Mary picking a winner or that horse coming from so far back to win. And still I couldn't take my eyes off the horses, slowing now, their bodies black with sweat, sides heaving, the white around their eyes showing not white any longer but red. Blood red. And I knew their hearts must feel like they were bursting and their lungs like they'd never get enough air.

Slowly the jockeys brought them to a walk, turned them so they were coming back towards me on their way to the paddock, and I saw the horses' faces were caked with the sandy soil of the track and I knew it must be thick in their nostrils and throats and I felt like I was choking myself.

What guts, I thought, giving themselves one hundred percent like that. I mean, what was in it for them? Nothing as far as I could see except maybe a drink of water and something to eat. Maybe a rest and then back to the track on another day and I wondered what it was in them that they'd give everything they had.

I turned away blinking, glad Mom and Mary weren't there to see me squinting like a fool.

"Got yourself a winner, son?" someone said and I turned and saw it was the guy who had lied about my age at the gate.

"My sister did. Sort of..." I answered.

"That right? She sure got lucky. That horse never won a race before."

"Yeah," I said. "I heard."

"You going to go help her collect her winnings?"

"She didn't bet," I said. "She's way too smart for that. See you."

I waved a hand his way and started running again thinking maybe I ought to tell Mary she should have. Bet some money, I mean. Could be betting's not that dumb after all. I mean, if she'd put just five bucks on that horse she'd have made...? I couldn't figure it out. Not with dodging people and running like I was. I'd just have to work on it some other time.

SIXTEEN

They were huddled over the tiny calculator in the palm of Mary's hand when I found them. One of Mary's finger nails, orange that day, brighter than a Gator T-shirt, was clicking away at the pin-sized buttons and numbers, mostly zeros, were flashing along the window at the top so fast you couldn't keep up with them. They didn't look up when I arrived, panting, but they spread out a bit and let me in and Mom's arm went up around my shoulder the way it always does to any of us, whether we've been gone five minutes out of the room or five months, like when Steve hasn't been able to get a ride home in a long, long time.

Right then though, Mary's nail was tapping away and she was saying, "Look, I'm showing you, Mom. If you put just a few dollars on this horse called Abacus and they pay thirty to one, you could at least cover your expenses for today. The parking. The admission. Look," she tilted the calculator and shaded it with her hand to be sure the sunlight wasn't stealing away any of her zeros and Mom was getting the full picture.

"I see what you're saying, honey. It's very interesting. But we're not here to throw money at horses. We're here..."

"To throw money at someone else's floor," Mary glowered, turning away in disgust.

"Oh, honey," Mom sighed. "I do know how you feel. That I'm a fool. That in my place you'd do things differently, but... I just won't give Harry the satisfaction of telling lies about me to those darling Aldersons. Not when I have it in my power, and in my bank account, to correct the situation." She reached for her purse. "Why don't you let Jeff run and get you a nice little sandwich, a nice big coke, and you can just sit here and relax. I know I'll find Al any minute now and then we can leave."

All the while she was talking she was rummaging in her purse, pulling out all the weird stuff she hauls around, until she got to the bank envelope stuffed with fifty dollar bills.

"Will you look at her," Mary hissed, lunging forward to cover with her body the money so carelessly held in Mom's hands. "She'll have us all mugged - murdered even - flashing all this money around. Give it to me, Mom. Tell her, Jeff. She can't be so careless."

"Yeah, give it to her, Mom," I agreed, taking the envelope from her and putting it in Mary's hand where right away it looked safer surrounded by the jagged spears of her gross-out nails.

Once, a few years back, a great big jerk of a guy was hassling me and my buddies off a basket ball court near our house, picking us up and tossing us aside so he could shoot some baskets, when Mary happened by. In two strides she was in that guy's face, snarling, spitting, screaming insults and he was backing off, then turning tail and heading for his car, so I know she's a match for any crook, or gang of crooks, that might be stupid enough to mess with her. You only had to look around at the crowd that day though to see that everybody was way too busy with their own programs and their own calculators to give us a thought.

"OK, Jeff," Mom said. "Now go get something really nice for Mary and then you can both relax till I get back."

"Never mind," Mary said, snatching the money from Mom's hand. "I'll go find something myself."

Watching her stride away, head tossing, a thousand dollars in her purse, I knew that, in spite of her frustration with Mom, Mary wasn't having such a bad day. In fact, in her own obnoxious way, Mary was having a blast, storing up bits of knowledge and information that later she'd exaggerate and turn into a really cool story for her friends, tying up the phone for hours and making them wish they'd been with her.

Turning back to Mom, I was about to ask what had been in the back of my mind ever since she got home yesterday. Yesterday? Jeez! Seemed a lot longer ago than that. But what I'd been wanting to ask about was Steve's car. I mean, if we were going back to broke again, how was she going to see herself as a woman of means and attract that car? Was she going to go for another thousand? And if so, wasn't she running out of time?

But I changed my mind. Didn't seem like that was the right time somehow.

"What about you?" she asked, turning to me now Mary was lost in the crowd. "Are you having fun?"

"Sort of," I nodded.

"But the horses?" she said. "I thought you'd love being around them."

"I do!" I said. "I'd like to be around them all the time. But I keep remembering you and Mary and why we came and it's like... It's just..."

"Too much?"

"Yeah," I said. "Way too much."

"Well, go then. Go and enjoy the day. Forget about the rest," she said, as though it was that easy.

"I'm glad Steve's not here," I said.

She nodded.

"He'd be coming right out of his tree," I said.

"Off the walls," she agreed.

We started to chuckle.

"He'd have an ulcer by now."

"He'd have all his hair torn out."

"He'd have chewed his nails to the quick."

"He'd be so mad at us."

By then we were laughing so hard we couldn't go on and I was feeling a lot better.

When we had quieted down some, Mom said, "The only trouble is, you're worrying too. Almost as bad as Steve would if he were here.

"Just don't," she went on. "Just look on it as a whole new learning experience or else I'll be worrying that you really are too young to be here. That all this," she waved towards the track and the betting windows, "isn't good for you. That I'm contributing to the delinquency of a minor, for heaven's sake!"

She stopped then because she saw she had really gotten to me.

"Here," she fished in her old wallet. "Here's ten. Go get yourself a hot dog and a cold drink and stop worrying. Your only responsibility today is to have fun. And check in here between every race, OK?"

"OK," I said, feeling for the first time that it really was OK. And feeling hungry. Oh, man... so hungry.

I bought a hot dog and a coke and looked around for a place to eat. I knew the horses had already gone down to the gate for the next race but with a really gloppy hot dog oozing mustard and ketchup in one hand, a drink in the other, I didn't feel like I could handle all the pushing and shoving and like I said, I was starved.

I decided to just sit out the whole race. Heck, there were plenty more to go. I found a bale of hay, though at the time I didn't know that's what it was called, just like I didn't know anything else about horses then, but I learned a lot that day and a lot more since, and that's what I sat on, a bale of hay, right near the stables.

If anything, the stable area was neater than all the other stuff I'd seen. It reminded me of when I was a little kid and had to go with Mom to the beauty parlor when she couldn't get a sitter. Only here it was horses everyone was fussing over, shampooing and brushing and braiding their manes, oiling their hooves, everyone hurrying and calling out to one other, like, "Hey, so and so's looking good today," the way the ladies used to say, "That cut is just darling, honey, just darling!" And you could tell here that no matter what they said, each groom thought his horse was better turned out than any of the others, just like you could tell that the ladies in the beauty parlor really thought everyone else's hair looked pretty trashed compared to what they were doing to their own customers.

I saw Suzy's Delight getting soaped down and hosed off. She looked exhausted. Her head drooped and she didn't seem to care too much what they did to her. But by the time they dried her off and covered her with a blanket and led her away, her ears were back up and her tail was swishing and she seemed ready to get out there and race again.

"Where're they taking her?" I asked a black kid hurrying by with a bucket of water in each hand.

"Ole Suzy? Suzy's gonna pig out," he said, putting the buckets down and flexing his fingers. "Gonna chow down."

"You work here?" I asked him.

"Ain't nobody works here," he said. "You work where your horse is at, man."

"Where's your horse at?"

"Where's my horse at?" he said, doing a sorry imitation of Eddie Murphy while he pointed across the paddock. "That's where my horse is at. That black dude over there. You know black is beautiful, right?"

"Yeah," I said. "I heard."

"You got it, man. That there is December Knight and that baby's gonna win us the fifth. See if he don't."

We walked towards December Knight while we talked and I hoped he wasn't noticing I was right there in the enclosure with him where I wasn't supposed to be. He put the buckets down and reached up and rolled back the horse's blanket.

"Look at the muscle, man," he said, running his hand down the horses neck and shoulders. "Look at the legs."

Without even thinking, I ran my hand down the horse's neck and was surprised at the sleek warm feel of it and at the rock hard strength under the softness and I thought, Hey, look at me! Standing here stroking a race horse just like I know what I'm doing. And I hated myself for the idiot smile I couldn't keep off my face. The same uncontrollable smile that always sneaks up on me when I'm trying to be my most cool.

"Got much more to do, Jim?" a voice behind us asked.

"No, sir, Mr. Winfield," Jim said, pulling the blanket back over December Knight in a big hurry. "We're ready to go, sir. Just showing my man here what kind of horse we're running in the fifth."

Him again! The guy from the gate. The guy from the finish line. He was smiling though. Nice friendly wrinkles around his eyes, hands in his pockets. Relaxed. Looking at his horse? Jeez, he owned this horse? No wonder the ticket lady forgot us when he came along.

"You shown your friend here any of our other horses?" he asked Jim.

"No, sir," Jim said, all indignant. "I been doin' my time with December here. Ain't had no time to go cruisin' with no..." Whatever he was going to call me, he changed his mind, and the sentence just hung there.

"Come along, then," Mr. Winfield said to me, "I'll show you around. Don't forget to have Bud bandage his legs up good," he called back to Jim. "I'm counting on you."

He showed me four horses all together. All of them his. But he knew every horse there and what they had done. He knew every owner, every jockey, every trainer. He talked to veterinarians and stable boys and blacksmiths. We went from one end of the paddock to the other and in and out of every stable. At first I was too awed to do much more than nod as he pointed things out to me but soon, because of his easy ways and his friendliness to everyone, and because the more he showed me, the more questions I had, I forgot to be tongue-tied and felt ten feet tall instead. I didn't remember the awe again until we were back beside December Knight where there was a whole bunch of people clamoring for his attention and I couldn't hardly believe I was part of the crowd.

The trainer, Joe Phelps, who I'd met back in the barn, was there and he was talking to the jockey, telling him not to push December Knight too soon, to let him settle down and hit his stride first. And there was another Joe who was crawling around adjusting the bandages that now covered the horses front legs from knee to fetlock - that's like a person's ankle - and then we all stood back a little while the trainer gave the jockey a leg-up. December Knight started acting nervous and one of the stirrups wasn't right and had to be adjusted and then Jim was leading them out to the gate and although December Knight danced sideways all the way, he went into the gate itself like it was no big deal.

"The hardest part of any race is waiting for that gate to go up," Mr. Winfield told me, leading me and the trainer to seats in the stands. But we'd hardly sat down than the gate was up and we were on our feet again.

"He came out clean," Joe Phelps said, following the field with his binoculars. I grabbed mine up quick and tried to adjust them but I was too excited and nervous and turned them the wrong way and decided to heck with it.

"Come on December Knight," I yelled, seeing the great black horse in about the middle of the pack.

"Keep him steady..." the trainer was muttering, "Easy does it..."

Mr. Winfield wasn't saying anything but he wasn't relaxed anymore. His arms were folded tight across his chest and his jaw was set.

When the horses streamed in front of us, they were still all bunched together, with December Knight right in the middle.

"He's got to get out of that huddle before the turn," Joe Phelps said and Mr. Winfield nodded. "Got to make his move." Then as they swept around the bend, he yelled, "Now, boy! Break away!"

I know there was no way that horse or that jockey could've possibly heard but at the very second the trainer spoke, December Knight seemed to drop back a pace or so and then he was coming up on the inside, fast, and we were all hollering.

As though December Night had been the instigator, the whole field spread out then and where they had been travelling fast before, now they were flying down the far side of the track as though there was some special reward in it for them and I wondered again what it was that could make a horse want to win so bad it would bust its gut trying.

"Heart," Mr. Winfield told me later when I thought to ask him. "That's what it means when you say a horse has heart. He wants to win. Wants to be the best. Heart is the difference between a fine horse and a champion. And you never know where you'll find it. Sometimes you can have the finest bloodlines and if your horse doesn't have heart all you've got is a looker out for a run in the sunshine. Your champion though, he's the one who's going to come through for you in rain and mud and when he's off color himself. He's got pride. He knows he's out there to win. It's in his blood and he'll die trying because he'll never, never give up. Same way it is with people," he concluded. "Same way and there aren't many around. So when you find one, you consider yourself lucky and you hang on to them because they'll stand by you when you need them."

I knew then, watching that race, that I was looking at a champion, or at least the makings of a champion, because that's what Mr. Winfield and Mr. Phelps said they had when December Knight streaked past the finish line a good two lengths ahead of the horse that came in second.

Seventeen

"I knew he had it in him," Joe Phelps said over and over again, while Mr. Winfield said, "What did I tell you? Didn't I tell you?"

When we got back to the paddock we were mobbed by people, all of them slapping Mr. Winfield and Mr. Phelps and the jockey on the back and saying stuff like, "Great horse. Great race. Great heart."

Jim looked like his face was going to crack he was grinning so hard and as he hurried forward to take charge of December Knight I gave him a high five.

"Black sure is beautiful," I told him.

"You got it, man," he said. "You got it."

I was going to follow him. Help him if he'd let me. Do anything so I could be around December Knight some more only right then Mr. Winfield turned to me and what he said really threw me.

"Your mother...." he began. And then he didn't say anything. Just stood there. And while I waited for him to go on, I started getting the idea that maybe he didn't know how to go on, and I couldn't hardly believe that. I mean, here's this guy whose horse just won this big race and everywhere we went you could tell people thought a lot of him and it just didn't seem possible that he was having a hard time with words like I do sometimes. And still the words didn't come and I just stood there, in arrested motion, kind've, like some kind of idiot.

Mr. Winfield must have guessed how I felt because he laughed suddenly and lost that look of uncertainty and touching my shoulder, said, "Let's go find your mother see if she had any money on my horse."

To be honest, I'd forgotten I had a mother and a sister and I realized I didn't even know who'd won the fourth and fifth races.

"I don't think so," I said, "My Mom's not here to watch the races and she freaks if you even mention gambling." And walking alongside of him, I amazed myself telling him Mom was really there to find a carpet guy. And then, I guess because he was so interested and because I liked him, I amazed myself some more telling him everything. I mean, about how Mom works but never has extra money and how she finally got some together so she could change her image but now she was going to give it all away over a dumb accident that could have happened to anyone.

The whole time I was talking Mr. Winfield was looking more and more surprised and kept saying, "I'll be damned." But he never did interrupt me and I suddenly realized we had stopped walking a while back and were just standing in the one place, me talking and him listening, his arms folded across his chest, like he was watching a race, one hand going up to stroke his chin every once in a while

"...and so," I finished, "that's how I know she wouldn't have bet any money on December Knight."

I looked up in the stands and saw Mom and Mary and it looked like they were arguing.

I pointed them out to Mr. Winfield and called out to Mom as we went up the steps because if they were getting into it, I needed them to stop. And also because I wasn't too sure how to handle the introductions and I wanted to warn Mom so she could help me out. She did.

She acted exactly as if she was welcoming him as a guest in our home. One she'd been expecting for a long time. How do adults do that, I wondered? She didn't even know the guy, hadn't been with us in the paddock to see how important he was and how everybody liked him and yet there she was with just the right things to say. I could have hugged her.

"The man from the gate!" she beamed, extending her hand and smiling. "I'm so glad Jeff found you." She slid sideways on the bench and patted the space she had vacated for him to sit down. "I'm afraid you must have thought us very rude running off earlier without a thank you, but frankly, that ogre at the gate had me quite rattled. Particularly since Jeff really is underage. But we're here on a really important mission and I was terrified she wasn't going to let him... us... in."

"So Jeff has been telling me," Mr. Winfield said, with a wink at me.

"Oh... I see..." Mom faltered a moment, wondering, I guess, just how much I had told him about the real reason we were there but she must have decided not to worry about it because she kept right on talking. "Mary and I were just...um... trying to decide what to do next," she said.

"And I'm telling her it's definitely time to go home now," Mary said, giving me a look that meant it's time to get her out of here.

I couldn't decide if she was telling me Mom had found Al and he'd told her to get lost or whether she'd already given him the money. Whatever the scenario, I didn't care. I was NOT about to go home.

There was what you'd call an uncomfortable silence. A lot of things needed to be said and Mom and Mary were not going to say them in front of Mr. Winfield. And he couldn't say anything either without letting them know I'd blabbed everything. It was up to me. I braced myself and asked a stupid question, "Did you have any money on December Knight?"

"Of course not!" Mom gasped. "You know I wouldn't dream..."

"Don't start, Mother," Mary warned, with a hasty look at Mr. Winfield who was being very careful not to look at anything in particular.

"Mr. Winfield..." I began. "Well... see... December Knight is his horse. And he owns a whole bunch of others," I added quickly, wanting to get across right away that he had money of his own and was not there to hit either one of them over the head and run off with their pocket books.

"Oh, my God," Mary gasped, forgetting to sing-song it. Unconsciously she sat up straighter and her arms relaxed around her purse.

"Well, my goodness," Mom said, and for a moment I thought she wasn't going to come through, but she did with, "How exciting!" and she extended her hand again and shook Mr. Winfield's. "Congratulations must be in order. Your horse won easily. I heard someone around here say this was his first race and that's why the odds against him were so high... um...so long?"

"That's right," Mr. Winfield smiled. "But they won't be next time he runs. Word gets around fast at the tracks. Next time he races you'll find the odds a lot shorter."

"Oh," Mom said. "Well then I'm doubly glad we saw him on his, uh... maiden voyage, so to speak. We've never been to a race track before and I doubt we'll ever come again..." She stopped and I knew she felt like she'd said too much.

"I already told him, Mom," I said. "I mean about the paint and looking for Al and your life savings and all."

"You did?" Mom gasped.

"What a jerk," Mary spat.

"From what Jeff's told me, you haven't had any luck so far finding this guy," Mr. Winfield said, smiling at Mom who looked really flustered.

"That's just it," Mary broke in. "I'm positive he's not here. And Mom forgot her glasses just like I knew she would.

She's already run up to two guys she thought were Al and one of them started following us till I told him where to go. Maybe next time I won't be so lucky. It makes me nervous carrying all this money around. It's time to go home. I hate family outings."

"Why don't you people stay with me for the rest of the day?" Mr. Winfield suggested. "Come with me over to my area. You won't be bothered over there."

"I think we should just go home," Mary insisted clutching her purse even tighter.

"No need for that," Mr. Winfield assured her. "You'll be fine with me."

I was awfully glad he was taking charge of Mom and Mary the way he was. I mean, I knew I wasn't going home until the last race was over and I also knew I'd have worried myself sick for the rest of the day if he hadn't been there.

"Come down to the paddock with me first," Mr. Winfield said, smiling at Mary and putting out a hand to help Mom to her feet. "I've got a horse running in the next race I'd like you all to take a look at."

"I'd love to, Mr. Winfield," Mom said. "But really, I must go on with my search."

"Surely a short time-out won't hurt," Mr. Winfield said. "And who knows, we might bump into him on our way. Failing that, you could try having him paged."

"You're right," Mom said. "And I really would love to see your horse, Mr. Winfield."

"David," he said, standing aside so Mom could go ahead of him down the steps. "The name is David."

"Get him," Mary said to me out of the corner of her mouth when they were several steps ahead of us. "The name is David," she mimicked.

"Don't you think he's cool?" I asked.

"He's cool, all right," Mary agreed. "A hunk is what he is."

"Wouldn't it be something if he liked Mom?" I breathed.

"Tell me about it. But he's got to have a wife somewhere."

"It was him that wanted to go find Mom," I said. "It wasn't my idea."

"Doesn't mean he's not married," Mary said.

"Yeah? Well where is she then?"

"Who knows. Home looking after the little ones, I bet."

"What little ones?"

"Jeez! How do I know? All I know is a guy that age has to have a wife and kids." Mary said. "That, or he's... uh... different."

"There's nothing different about him," I said emphatically, thinking, God, but she can get on my nerves the way she can't take anything or anyone at face value but has to re-invent them into a story she'll blab to her friends later.

As soon as we got in the paddock I lined myself up next to Mr. Winfield and Mom and stayed as far away from Mary as I could get.

His horse in the next race, the seventh, was a gray. A filly he called it. Mom said she thought she was beautiful and

Mary said what a pretty face it had and they embarrassed me so bad I took off to talk to Jim.

"Who's the chick with The Man?" he wanted to know, nodding toward Mary.

"That's my sister," I said.

"That's some sister," he said, grinning.

"She's a pain in the butt," I said.

"That's some pain in the butt," he said. "And who's the other one?"

"That's my Mom."

"Yeah? The Man and your Mom are friends?"

I wished I could have given him a "yes" instead of just a vague kind of shrug. If they were friends I'd get to be around him and his horses all the time. Maybe even learn to ride.

I looked over to where they were all standing talking. Mom was saying something to Mr. Winfield and he was watching her close like it was something real interesting and then they were laughing and he touched her shoulder and pointed something out to her and they started walking towards whatever it was.

"Is he married?" I asked Jim.

"Not no more, he ain't. His old lady up and left a couple years back."

"Where'd she go?"

"Went off to visit their son up in New York someplace and never did come back. Said she didn't want to see another horse or paddock or race track the rest of her life."

"No way! Think she'll ever come back?"

"Hell, no! My Momma say good thing too. Say she shoulda gone a long time back. Her and the boy both."

"Yeah? Well, like... What was wrong with them?"

"Just they liked city ways, I guess. Both always looking for excuses to get off the farm. Here, hand me that brush beside you. You got me talking so bad I ain't getting this horse ready. Dammit, boy, either help me out or go see your Momma."

We got busy then. At least Jim did. I just handed him the things he needed.

"This filly's skittish," Jim said as the horse fidgeted under his brushes. "But fast. Get her to pay attention and she'll beat the best. We brought her down today so's she could get some real experience but the man say next year's gonna be her year, don't he, babe?" The gray rubbed her head against Jim's shoulder.

"See," he grinned. "She say, 'You got it, man'."

Mom and Mary and Mr. Winfield came over then and the jockey came out with the saddle and I didn't think they were ever going to get it on the filly at all the way she kept swinging away from them and I looked at the jockey thinking, Sooner you than me, dude! But he just stood there, arms folded, looking bored until they finally got the saddle on, then that little guy was on board so fast I didn't think the filly even noticed, but it blew my mind the change in her. As soon as he hit the saddle and took up the reins, he started talking to her, kind of stern at first, then softer, and it seemed like she understood just what he said and settled down as though she trusted him. He took her out of the paddock and down to the gate as nice as you please. She wasn't too happy about going into the gate though and Mr. Winfield told Jim to get on down there and stand by in case he was needed. But the jockey must have said the right thing again because by the time Jim got there, she was in the gate and it shot up and we had to run to get back to our seats.

"You should have put a couple of bucks on her, Mom," I said, watching her streak out ahead of the rest of the field.

"Maybe I should have," Mom agreed, more, I knew to get across to Mr. Winfield that she thought he had a nice horse than to actually wish she had.

"Your mother saved her money, son," Mr. Winfield said. "That filly came out of the gate way too fast. She thinks she can run all day and all night and she can't. She'll learn though. Give her time."

He was right. By the time the field passed in front of us she was losing ground and by the time they were opposite, on the other side of the track, she was second from last. I yelled for her anyway. We all did. And as they came into the last corner before the homestretch, she tried, picking up a little, but she didn't have it in her and finished last.

"Spends herself too soon," the trainer said.

"Give her a year," Mr. Winfield said again. "Come back in a year and you'll see her coming in first every time she runs. I'll stake my reputation on it."

EIGHTEEN

"You want to back a winner," Mr. Winfield told Mom, pointing to a number on her program, "put your money on my horse in this next race."

"Yes, go on, Mom," Mary said. "Do something wild for once in your life. Which one is it?"

"Number One," Mr. Winfield grinned. "And number one he should be, too. If ever I've bred a winner, that's him. Gallant Fighter. His sire is what made my stables what they are today and this is the dam's first colt. Best two year old I ever ran. I'm counting on this horse to win me the Derby same as his daddy did before him."

"The Kentucky Derby?" I yelped.

"That's right," he said. "Maybe even the triple crown."

"Wow..." I breathed.

"Give me all your money Mom," Mary said. "I'll go put it on him. You can get that whole house refloored if you want."

"Hold on just a minute, young lady," Mr. Winfield said, but he was laughing. "Your mother is right, gambling is gambling. I had more in mind just a ten or something on that order. After all, from what Jeff has told me, your mother worked hard for that money. My stables would be proud knowing that a few of those dollars was riding on its star."

"Make it a twenty, Mom," I said. "In fact, if I were you, I'd put fifty on him."

We were all looking at Mom then and she was wasn't too happy about it. She looked from the program to David Winfield and I knew, watching her, that she didn't want to put any money on Gallant Fighter but at the same time, she wanted to show support for Mr. Winfield's horse.

"What have you got to lose, Mom?" I said, looking at her and hoping that Mr. Winfield wouldn't guess I was pleading.

"She's not going to lose a dime," Mr. Winfield said quickly. "If I thought there was a chance in hell any other horse in this race could beat him I wouldn't let her put down one dollar. That's why he's running two to one. Everyone here knows he's the hands-down winner."

"You're right," Mom said, smiling up at him and letting me know with a quick look she was in on this with me. "Put five on him please, Mary."

"Five?" Mary squawked. "Mom, you know he's going to win. At two to one you could walk away with a bundle. You could give old Al his bribe money and still..." she paused, "be a lady of means."

"That's enough, Mary," Mom said quickly. "No need to bore Mr. Winfield with the state of our finances. Put five on him, please."

"I'll come with you, Mary, show you the ropes." Mr. Winfield said. "And Jeff, you stay here with your mother till I get back."

I looked at Mary's canvas bag lying between us on the bench and, feeling suddenly responsible, moved closer to Mom so that it was wedged tight between us. "Somebody could come along and rip this whole thing off." I said. "Did you stop to think about that?"

"Jeff! Jeff!" Mom said, laughing. "You've been watching too much TV. Stop worrying. Nobody's going to rip us off."

"They better not try," I said. Then, "You don't think his horse is going to win this race, do you?"

She shook her head and sighed. "What do I know? I just don't like hearing about sure things. Sure winners. Knowledge makes me nervous. I'd sooner go on intuition. Not knowing a thing," she shrugged. "That doesn't mean it won't win though."

"Do you like him?" I asked, thinking if I changed the subject fast I might catch her off guard.

Mom nodded. "What's not to like?"

"Would you go out with him if he asked you?"

"If he's single, I would. "

"He is," I said. "I suppose now you're going to tell me you imagined him too."

She nodded her head. "As a matter of fact, I did. Not necessarily him or meeting him today, but I always knew I'd meet someone just like him. I've imagined it far too long for it not to happen.

"I wonder where he lives?" I said dreamily.

"In Florida someplace. Hush, here they come. Mary looks beautiful today, doesn't she?"

I looked at Mary for maybe the billionth time in my life, trying to see what it was made other people's heads turn when she walked by and suddenly I saw her as though I was a stranger and for a moment I couldn't believe she was my sister and I'd never seen it before. She caught me staring at her then and said, "What're you staring at, moron?" And as I looked, whatever it was, was gone. She was the same old Mary, my sister, and I couldn't stand being around her.

"Is it OK if I go back down to the paddock and help Jim now you're back?" I asked Mr. Winfield.

He looked startled and said, "Why, that's fine with me Jeff, but shouldn't you check with your Mother?" I felt myself turning red then, realizing I'd treated him like he had more authority than my own mother. I looked at Mom but she didn't seem to notice.

"You're too late, honey," was all she said. "Look, they're in the gate."

"Which is Gallant Fighter?" I asked, seeing the now familiar surge of horses and jockeys, hearing the wonderful drum of hooves.

"Second from the fence on the inside," Mr. Winfield said, already on his feet. "The chestnut."

I hope Mom's wrong, I thought, watching the chestnut streaking along with two other horses. I hope she's dead wrong. I looked over at her and she was sitting rolling and unrolling her program, not really wanting to watch the race.

"He's gonna win," I hissed in her ear.

"I hope so," she murmured. "I really do."

But he didn't. At the half-way point a gray got half a length ahead of him and stayed there through the finish line.

He was well named, that Gallant Fighter, I'll say that for him. He fought all the way. You could see him straining everything he had to pass the gray.

"He lost it at the second turn," Mr. Winfield said at last when the horses had left the track and the silence in our group was about to get unbearable. "He rushed it and let himself get boxed in."

"It's only one race," Mom said. "He's got plenty more ahead of him."

"You can tell he's a champion," Mary said uncertainly. "At least, I could."

On a deep sigh, Mr. Winfield said, "I do believe I feel worse about you losing your money than I do about my horse." He reached into his inside jacket pocket for his wallet. "Although, of course, I insist on reimbursing you."

Old Mom was on her feet in a flash grabbing at his sleeve. "You'll do no such thing," she said. "This has been a very good lesson for my children. With all the money they've seen changing hands here today, I wouldn't want them getting the idea that any time they're running short all they have to do is go to the nearest race track. They needed to know, we all did, that it's as easy to lose as it is to win. They also needed to know that when you lose at anything, or make a mistake, as I did yesterday, you take responsibility for it. But thanks. That was a very kind offer."

Mr. Winfield looked at Mary and me from under his eyebrows a moment, then shrugged. "Your mother is right, of course. But I'd feel a lot better if you'd learned your lesson from somebody else's horse and not mine." He smiled when he said that but it was like some of Mom's smiles, phony. "Come on, Jeff," he turned to me. "Let's get down there and see what our jockey has to say. That horse should have won, dammit. He was ready."

We left Mom and Mary then and it wasn't until a long time later when I heard the loudspeaker overhead asking a Mr. Al Harding to report to the track office that I remembered and knew it was Mom having our Al paged and I hoped, if he was there, he'd ignore the page. Meanwhile, Mr. Winfield and his people got really involved in why they'd lost the race. They even drew a circle of the track in the dirt and crouched over it trying to figure out where and why they'd lost. Jim and two other guys from Mr. Winfield's stables were getting Gallant Fighter and the other horses ready for the long ride home. I helped as best I could. I couldn't hardly believe all the stuff they'd brought with them. Jim had a checklist with him and he had to find every thing on it and get it all loaded before they could even begin with the horses.

"Stay cool, man," Jim said, giving me five when the list was complete and the last of the horses had gone up the ramp into the van and were bolted in. "Tell The Man to bring you up see us sometime."

"I'll do it," I said. "I mean, like... I'll try."

The paddock seemed boring when I turned back to it. There were only a few horses left, the ones that were running in the last race, I guessed. Shadows were lengthening and a little wind had picked up and was blowing bits of trash around. It felt like it might get cold in the night - some late cold front from up north straying our way – and I hoped it would. We don't get many cold days or nights in Florida and I love them.

Once, when I was a real little kid, Mom woke me up one morning all excited. "Come look at this," she'd said, clacking up the shades. "It's snowing!" And it was! Little tiny flakes fluttering out of a gray sky. I'd gone tearing out of the house just like I was, bare feet and pajamas, and scraped up a handful off the driveway which was the only place it settled. There hadn't been enough to do much with but we put together enough to make a couple of real little snowballs and quick put them in one of those plastic freezer bags and stuck 'em in the freezer.

They're still there. And every year since I've been wishing for another snow so I could scoop some of that up, too, and have me a vintage snow collection. Hasn't happened yet though...

Nineteen

It wasn't that cold of a day at the track though. That day the sun was going down a bright clear red in a pale blue sky with just enough chill in the air to make you wish you had a wind-breaker and think about hot chocolate.

David Winfield was still talking to some people I didn't know and I wondered if I should go over and tag along or go find Mom and Mary. He looked totally wrapped up in his conversation though and didn't notice me when I walked right by him. It made me feel kind've unimportant and I thought maybe I'd really gotten carried away earlier thinking I'd get to know him better and maybe visit him in his big house – for sure he'd live in a big house - and maybe learn to ride and all. Well, damn... I started feeling really low and wondered how I could have ever been that stupid.

"Where's Mom?" I asked Mary, coming up on her alone in the stands. She didn't look any too happy either, sitting all huddled up and grouchy-looking.

"She keeps coming and going," she said, sounding seriously ticked-off. "Said she was going to the restroom this last time out."

"Did old Al What's-his-name ever answer that page?"

"Nope."

"What's the matter with you?"

"Everything... This whole wasted day... I'm freezing... I'm hungry... Depressed..."

"That's it?"

"It's enough, isn't it? Just thinking that Monday we'll all be back in our dumb routines: Mom's dramas. Work. Car payments. And well... There's other ways to live too, you know. Only we don't get to live them."

I knew what she meant. It was like we'd opened a door to a magic kind of place only we wouldn't get to stay.

"We did get to visit though," I reminded her. "Don't forget that."

She sighed. "Big deal. Seems to me we'd have been better off not knowing anything about it. I mean, what have we accomplished, huh? Zip."

We were quiet a good long while after that, each lost in our own thoughts. It was me who broke the silence, asking, "You think he'll come back up here? Mr. Winfield, I mean."

"Why would he?" Mary scowled. "He's got it all, hasn't he? Horses. Friends. Money. Looks. Why would he come looking for us?"

I shivered. "Want me to go see if I can find some hot chocolate?" I asked, feeling like I wanted to do something nice for her for once.

Mary's face brightened. "Yeah. Great idea. And something to eat, too. Here, you got any money?" she reached for her purse but came up with Mom's. "Damn," she said. "She's done it again. Taken off with my pur..." and suddenly she was on her feet, her face whiter than white paper.

"It's got all her money in it," she hissed. "All of it."

"So what?" I said, but I was on my feet too, pulled up by the panic in her face and voice. "What's the big deal? You're the one put it there, remember?"

"You know her! Why do you think I took it away from her in the first place? You know how she forgets things. She'll lay it down someplace and walk away without it or..."

"Not today, she won't." I interrupted. "You think she'd spend this whole day trying to track down this Al guy and then walk off and leave her life savings in a restroom? 'Course she won't. She's not that stupid." But I was worried. With a Mom like ours, who knew?

"If you'd seen her face when she took off this last time you'd know she could too be that stupid. She was like, dazed. A zombie. I figure it was when no one answered that page and she knew we were running out of time, she just, like, folded."

"Yeah? Well, no wonder. I mean, who wouldn't?" I sat back down and in my mind worked my way through the sorry checklist of Mom's troubles: a house she'd really worked on an ugly mess, it's owners - right then probably - staring horror-struck at what she'd done. Harry in the background blabbing what a fool he'd been hiring Mom in the first place, but not to worry, he'd see it was all put right even if it meant taking her to court. Then wasting a whole day chasing around a race track looking for a guy who'd probably never even showed. Jeez!

Plus, like Mary said, Monday morning wasn't far off. Only this Monday Mom wasn't going to have a job to rush off to and we'd have to go through all that grief. Again! Worse than all that, she'd be beating herself over the head and driving us crazy trying to figure how she'd "thought" herself into such a mess.

But then suddenly I brightened. "If she never found Al," I said, "that means she never gave him the money. At least she's still got that."

"She'd have given him that money over my dead body," Mary snarled. "Why else do you think I came here today?"

I felt a big rush of admiration for Mary then, picturing Mom all flustered, wringing her hands, pleading, getting ready to hand over her life savings and Mary stepping in, taking it from her, looking Al right in the eye and saying something really cool, like, "...and of course, you'll see Harry gets the bill, right?"

I was just trying to think of some kind of compliment to pay Mary – nothing too over the top, of course, wouldn't have wanted her getting shot on herself – to let her know it felt good having her around sometimes, like, once in a while, when she scared me spitless again, saying, "What if someone snatches her purse?"

"Let's just go find her," I said. "There can't be that many ladies rooms around here. We... You'll just have to go in all of them. Which one's the closest?"

"The one over by the betting windows," she said, pointing. And then her lips formed a big, silent "O" and she looked at me without seeing me at all and then she grabbed my hand and we were clattering and stumbling down the steps of the stands which wasn't easy on account of a lot of people were going the other way, and a bunch of others were on their feet, yelling, because the gate had gone up on the last race of the day.

"Where are we going?" I yelled but she didn't answer. Hadn't even heard me.

When we got to the bottom she stopped and didn't seem to know which way to go.

"Dammit," I said. "What is with you?"

But the fight seemed to have gone out of her and she slumped down on the bottom step as though her legs couldn't hold her up anymore. She cupped her hands around my ear and said, "It's too late to stop her now anyway."

"From going to the bathroom?"

"From betting, stupid. She's gone and bet on that last race. I just know she has. That's why she took my purse."

"Now it's you losing it," I sneered. "What makes you think she'd up and do a dumb thing like that? She wouldn't. You heard her. She thinks betting's for the birds. Who wouldn't after the way Mr. Winfield's horse went and proved it for all time! You're nuts!"

"You don't understand," Mary wailed. "She has. She's gone and bet everything. I know she has."

"What do you mean, everything?" I said, feeling as dumb as she always says I am.

"I mean, EVERYTHING!" Mary howled, looking like she was about to cry. "Her whole freaking thousand."

My mouth went dry in the weirdest way when she said that and nothing would come out of it, but I shook my head, No! Shook it hard again refusing to believe my mother would go and do a stupid, dumb-ass thing like that. All of it? On one horse? Never. No way. Not in a million years. She just wouldn't. I mean... why would she?

"What makes you think she'd do that?" I finally managed to whisper. "Why're you saying all this?"

"Because... just before she left for the restroom she was muttering something about how everything in life boils down to not being afraid. How if you believe in yourself, trust your instincts, you don't hold back. You do what you have to do. And when this day was over she wanted to know that for once in her life she'd done just that - been fearless. Don't you get it? This isn't about betting on a horse. It's about her taking a stand. She's betting on herself."

"That's a pretty gutsy thing to do," I marveled. "Even if it is nutty. Poor Mom, feeling she had to prove herself like that, I mean. Which horse?"

"Beats me," Mary said, unrolling her program and smoothing it out. We studied the list of names, all those weird and crazy-sounding names for those incredible animals: Follow Me Home, Cat's Meow, Feather Spin, Land 'o Dawn, Grace, Bold Man's Wife, Godfather, Timpani...

The names danced before our eyes, meaningless to us. What had sparked her, I wondered. What could have made her do such an improbable, wild and unlikely thing? And then it jumped out at me. The name. The only name it could possibly be.

"That's the one," I said to Mary, stabbing my finger at Bold Man's Wife.

"How come? How do you know?" she babbled, looking wildly from me to the program.

"Are you blind? Look at it," I said, almost choking, wanting to explain yet at the same time wanting her, for once in her life, to have to ask me how I knew something she didn't.

"What? Tell me! I don't get it."

"Look at it again," I said, feeling suddenly wise and very patient, knowing I had her. And when she still didn't get it, I said, "Look at the initials, dumb-dumb. B-M-W, Bold Man's Wife. Same as the car. She's doing it for Steve's car! She always said she'd get a clue. See something somewhere or hear something and just KNOW. Now do you get it?"

Mary groaned and buried her face in her hands and I have to tell you I didn't have the guts to even stand up, never mind look towards the track. I knew, though, that the horses had to be coming into the corner on the far side of the track, coming into the fourth and final turn. Was a horse with the initials of a car up there in front? Was it? I put my head down on my knees, scrunched up my shoulders and put my hands over my ears. I didn't want to hear. Didn't want to know.

The crowd around us was on their feet then, the names of the lead horses on their lips: Follow me Home. Timpani. And yes! Someone was hollering for Bold Man's Wife. She was in the running then. But which one was she?

We didn't even know what she looked like! Was she a bay? A chestnut? Black? Gray? I pushed my fingers harder into my ears, and then suddenly I was on my feet and Mary was, too, and we were running and shoving our way up to the rail.

"Damn kids," somebody snarled.

"Up yours, buster!" Mary snarled and I saw again from the corner of my eye the big guy with the cigar from earlier, and then the horses were thundering by with not more than fifty yards to go to the finish line.

"There's a couple of them in the lead," I yelled up to Mary from where I knelt looking through people's legs.

"But which one is she?" she screamed.

Like how was I supposed to know? She think I was some kind of psychic? I stood up and gave the guy in front of me a terrific shove, trying to make it look like somebody'd shoved me and I couldn't help it, and got my shoulder in between him and the guy next to him. "Just a cotton-picking minute here," he spluttered, but I'd slid through, at least the top half of me had, and I saw the glistening rumps of the horses streaming by and then, for no reason I could see, one of the lead horses went down, his jockey landing in a crumpled heap nearby, and the rest of the field was veering to get around both and streaming on past the finish line.

"Which horse went down? What happened?" I yelled to the faces around me, some looking disgusted, some happy. Nobody answered. The man I had shoved grinned wickedly and stepped back quickly so I fell to my knees, but as I was going down I heard someone - the loudspeaker guy? - say, "Hold on to your betting slips, ladies and gentlemen, pending the judges' decision on the outcome of the last race," and Mary was dragging me to my feet yelling, "Judge's decision!" like it was the major disaster of all time.

"What's it mean?" I gasped, brushing grass and dirt off my knees.

"Dunno... Must mean..." she shrugged.

"One of the horses went down," I said. "It's got to be about that. We need to find out which one. You suppose it could've been..." I hated to say the name, "that Bold... you know... BMW horse? Oh, God! Don't let it be her."

The crowd was thinning out, those remaining looking from their betting slips to the loudspeaker, waiting, I figured, for it to tell them what to do next. On the track we could see the horse that went down was still down and a bunch of men – veterinarians? – were crowded around it, a couple of them kneeling, checking out its legs, looking in its mouth.

Next to them, an ambulance had pulled up and guys in white jackets were loading the jockey onto a stretcher.

"You think they're going to be OK?" I gasped, realizing only after I spoke that I was talking to the guy I'd shoved earlier. The one who'd brought me to my knees.

"Sure," he said, seeming friendlier. "Jockeys know how to fall. Know to roll when they hit the dirt."

"I meant the horse," I spluttered. "What about the horse? Is it OK?"

"If it broke a leg, it ain't. It broke a leg, they'll shoot it."

I heard Mary let out a noise between a gasp and a moan.

"That's right," the guy went on. "A horse breaks its leg, there's no way to fix it. Carries too much weight, see. Bones can't set." He made a face. "It's how come they shoot 'em."

"Not here," Mary blubbered, looking green. "They wouldn't shoot it here, would they?"

"Nah," the guy said, looking around. "Too many people. Wouldn't look good. What they'll maybe do is give it a tranquilizer, keep it down, put it in the horse ambulance, haul it out back, see what's what." He looked at his watch, touched his head in a kind of salute and started walking away.

Mary and I turned to look at the horse and saw the men around it stepping back while others put a tarp down and worked at rolling the horse onto it.

I felt a lump the size of an ostrich egg fill my throat and tears burn and film my eyes. I turned away quickly and saw the guy we'd just talked to was still only a few feet away.

"Hey," I called, my voice sounding weird over the lump, "you know which horse that was went down? Its name, I mean?"

"Bold Man's Wife," he called back, shaking his head in a do-you-believe-it kind of way. "Heard the rumor she was a winner. Put my whole paycheck on her. Would've made thirty grand she'd come in first." Very deliberately he held up his betting slip, tore it in half, watched the pieces float to the ground, scuffed dirt over them and went on his way.

I looked at Mary knowing she had to be thinking the same thing I was: that if Mom had gone and done what we thought she'd done, she'd lost in more ways than one.

I opened my mouth to say we needed to go find her, when the loudspeaker crackled overhead and THE VOICE said, "Ladies and Gentlemen, thank you for your patience. The judges have reviewed the photo-finish between Follow Me Home and Timpani in the last race and the winner, by the narrowest of margins is Timpani. I repeat, the winner is Timpani."

There were whoops and hugs from some of the people waiting around, boos and disgusted faces from others.

"Poor Mom," I said. "Think how she must feel. For once in her life she goes and does something really wild and reckless and now..."

Mary drew in a deep breath, all set to come up with something really blistering, but she let it go on a sigh and said instead, "Yeah. I wouldn't want to be her."

"We've got to go find her," I said.

Mary shook her head. "I don't think she'll want to be found. Not yet anyway. Not till this is over. Maybe not ever."

"Let's go find Mr. Winfield then," I suggested, feeling like I could really take being around someone who wasn't going to get hysterical on me.

Again Mary shook her head. "Let's just leave him out of this."

"But he might leave! That was the last race."

"So he leaves. There's nothing we can do about it."

Feet dragging we made our way back up through the thinning crowd to the seats that had been ours off and on all day and what it felt like to me was that I'd spent my whole life there. That I'd never lived - not really lived - anyplace else. And I remember thinking how the events of the day were changing all of us. That the people who walked back into our house that night would be way different from the ones that walked out that morning. I mean, I knew we'd look the same and act the same and all our friends would think we were the same, but we'd be different. Forever different.

I don't remember which one of us saw her first, but out of nowhere there was Mom coming slowly towards us looking like she'd just been run over by something big. I mean, really, really big.

"She looks awful," Mary said to me, and to Mom, "It's OK, Mom. Whatever it is you've done, it's going to be OK. We'll work it out. Just come sit down."

Dazedly Mom ran her fingers through her hair which looked damp and messy and said, "I had to do it, you know. Just had to."

"'Course you did," Mary shrugged. "I mean, why not? There was your clue. You took a chance. Too bad it didn't work out..."

But Mom wasn't listening, just kept right on talking as though Mary hadn't spoken.

"I mean, knowing what I knew I just couldn't not, could I? I had to tell someone otherwise I wouldn't have been able to live with myself. Not ever..."

Together Mary and I stared at her in total confusion.

"What are you talking about?" Mary exploded.

"Who did you tell?" I asked - more like yelped. "What did you tell?"

"I told a cop, of course! I mean... a policeman. I could see he didn't believe a word I was saying. He told me I probably just bumped into the vet or a blacksmith. But I kept right on talking – yelling, actually - and finally he said something into his walkie-talkie and it said something back, I didn't catch what, and then he said, 'Thank you ma'am,' and took off running and now..."

"Mo-om..." we interrupted, again. "What are you talking about? What did you tell the cop? What happened?"

Again, she didn't hear a word we said, just kept right on going, "If we'd gone home and I hadn't acted, it would have been just one more example of me running scared. Thinking I had no right to be so bold when I was already in more trouble than I could handle; that I'd be living proof of what you always say I am, Mary, a wimp. All talk and no action. And there was this horse in the last race, and its initials came out to..."

"B-M-W," we chorused. "We know."

"You do? You noticed too?" she snapped. "How could you? You see... Well, I just couldn't believe it. There it was. The clue I'd been looking for all these months. Only... I couldn't figure what I was supposed to do about it. I mean, what? So I just started walking around, thinking... wondering... And then I thought I ought to maybe go take a look at this horse. You know, in the paddock, and maybe it would come to me there and I..."

"Put everything on her," Mary finished for her. "All the Al money."

"I'd never do that," Mom screeched. "You know I wouldn't! I was just looking at her and she was so, so beautiful... And then I saw a couple of creeps I'd seen earlier and they were yelling and cussing at the horse's groom like you wouldn't believe! What I couldn't understand was why nobody was telling them to shut up and go away.

"I guess everyone was too busy with their own horses to pay attention," she shrugged. "Else listening to the commentary on the ninth race - it was a real close finish from what I could make out... And meantime, the creeps were shaking their fists at the groom and yelling something about reporting the groom and the horse's owner to the Stewards and they took off.

"Coming out of the paddock they walked right in front of me and that's when I heard what they were saying..." she shook her head in disbelief. "I just couldn't believe it. I thought, They couldn't have... They wouldn't! In broad daylight? It was just all so outrageous it made me wonder if it was me who'd made a mistake. Not hearing them right, I mean... Not understanding... I even wondered if it was some kind of clue... You know, another..."

"Mom..." I interrupted through clenched teeth, "get to the point. What did they say?"

"Yes, what?" Mary spluttered. "What? Tell us... Now!"

"I am! Let me finish! Well... I was just so confused by then I knew I had to sit quietly for a minute and think things through and I went back up in the stands to you, Mary..."

Mary nodded, opened her mouth to speak, but Mom didn't notice.

"... I'd no sooner sat down," she rattled on, "than I knew I had to do something, say something to somebody or go crazy so I hurried back down and what do I see? The same two jerks heading for the betting windows.

"You should have seen them!" she said with a shudder. "They were so gross! Laughing like fools... Elbowing each other in the ribs... Pulling huge wads of hundred dollar bills out of their pockets... And then one of them dropped something!" she paused, eyes widening. "His buddy cussed him out and snatched it up quick but not before I saw what it was and knew for sure I had been right. Now do you see why I had to tell someone?"

"No!" Mary snapped. "How could we when we don't even know what he... they... dropped. Or what they said..."

"Took me forever to find a cop," Mom gasped. "And by the time I told him, the gate had gone up and, Oh!... the thought of that poor horse." She shuddered, moaned. "Now do you..."

"Mom," Mary interrupted in her sternest voice. "Sit down! You're not making any kind of sense. You need to just be still and not say another word until you can get things straight in your own head. Then you can tell us from the beginning. Take your time. We've got all day. Kind've..."

Like a sleep walker Mom sat where Mary and I put her and what I was thinking was, OK for Mary telling her to take her time. But me, I needed to know what the heck was going on. Like, right then.

"Where were you anyway," I began. "You look awful. Where have you been?"

"I was in the restroom," she said sheepishly, "...throwing up."

"You should have come and got us." Mary snapped. "Anyway, you should be very, very happy. We thought you'd gone and put your life savings on that BMW horse. Lucky thing you didn't. You saved yourself a bundle. Didn't you hear the loudspeaker? A couple other horses got into a photo-finish. Timpani won. That BMW horse was out of it. She went down..."

Mom drew in her breath in a horrified moan and forgetting what Mary had told her about chilling out, was back on her feet, ready to start in all over again when we saw Mr. Winfield coming up the steps towards us with a cop and what he said shut us all up pretty darn quick, I tell you what!

"Is this the woman you were telling me about, Officer?" was what he said.

"Yes, sir, Mr. Winfield," the cop answered. "That's the one." Turning to Mom he said, "Ma'am, I need you to come with me, please. Detective Johnson and the stewards need to take a statement from you... Set the record straight..."

"But..." Mom spluttered, all aghast and looking at Mr. Winfield as though he owed her an explanation. "I only know what I already told you and really, I... I have to leave now. I have to find a man... I mean, I came here to look for a man. That is..."

Mr. Winfield held out his hand to help Mom to her feet. "It won't take long," he said reassuringly. "We just want to get it in writing now we've got them. Because of your quick thinking, we've been able to nab two of the worst crooks on the circuit. There are warrants out for their arrest all up and down the eastern seaboard. We all owe you a huge debt."

Totally mystified, jaws dropping, Mary and I looked from one another to Mom to Mr. Winfield to the cop wondering just what in heck Mom had gone and done.

Mr. Winfield laughed at the expression on our faces. "I'll explain everything," he said, "while your mother is giving her statement. It's all quite simple, really. You're going to be very proud of her."

As soon as Mom and the cop left, Mr. Winfield sat down between Mary and me and filled us in. Seemed there were these two guys – real scumbag kind've guys – making a lot of trouble and causing a lot of grief in the racing world going around slipping drugs into promising winners just before they ran their races. Drugs that could shut a horse down if given at just the right time before a race so that at the moment the horse was at maximum thrust – like, giving its all to cross the finish line, heart pumping, lungs bursting, blood coursing – the drug kicked in and Bam, they were out of it. Sometimes the horses lived to race again. Sometimes they didn't.

"What about the BMW horse," Mary or I interrupted, "is she going to be OK?

"Too soon to say right now," Mr. Winfield answered, "Vets are working on her right now. We'll know by morning..."

Shaking his head in disgust, he went on with his explanation. Seems these guys had gotten away with it as long as they had because they were small-time owners themselves, running a couple of horses – nags, Mr. Winfield called them – which gave them entrée into the stable and paddock area where they could perform their dirty little deed with nobody suspecting it was an inside job.

All they needed to pull it off was a split-second of inattention on the part of a horse's entourage and their job was done. They'd engineer that opportunity themselves by one of them creating a diversion, like accusing someone of moving their tack-box or saddle or crowding them, so the other could deliver the goods, a sugar cube laced with the drug being their usual method.

"But how could Mom have known about all that?" I asked as Mr. Winfield concluded his explanation. "I mean, she's never been near a race track her whole life."

"Your mother is a very observant woman," Mr. Winfield said. "As well as an intuitive one. She noticed the two guys in question when we were all in the paddock earlier. Pointed them out to me, as a matter of fact, saying one of them needed a haircut so bad he looked like a horse himself from the rear. We'd laughed about it."

"I remember seeing you guys cracking up," I said.

Mr. Winfield nodded. "Right," he said. "Then later, when she was trying to figure out what she was supposed to make of both her "clue" and what she'd seen and overheard, she saw them heading for the betting windows and followed them.

"Somewhere in there one of the guys dug a bit too deep in his pocket and a couple of sugar cubes hit the ground. As soon as she saw that, she knew she had heard them right and reported them."

"But what did she hear?" Mary interrupted.

"Initially, she heard one of them ask the other if he'd been able to deliver the goods and if the horse had swallowed it down. 'Like feeding candy to a baby,' the other guy said with a self-satisfied smirk.

"Then later, at the betting windows, she heard the bragging of cowardly idiots," Mr. Winfield continued. "Trash talk like, 'Another sure fire winner bites the dust, huh? So long Bold-whatever-the-hell-your-name-is... Was!'

"Got careless is what they did," Mr. Winfield concluded. "One of them did, anyway. Took the rest of the world for fools." He grinned. "Didn't figure on a smart lady with some horse savvy putting two and two together and coming up with four the way your mother did."

"I still don't get what could have tipped her off," Mary pouted. "Nothing they said or did would have meant a thing to me. I'd have just taken them for a couple of jerks and looked the other way."

Mr. Winfield shrugged. "They were making a scene around *her* horse, remember? The one she believed to be her "clue". That got her protective instincts up. And don't forget she once owned a horse, knows that sugar to a horse is as irresistible as drugs to an addict. When those sugar cubes hit the ground she had all the proof she needed. On top of that, she knew they had already done their dirty work and she was beside herself with worry.

"What impresses me is that she followed through on her hunch and had the guts to act on her suspicions. She hadn't made the kind of scene she did – the officer said she went berserk - those two scumbags'd be doing the same thing someplace else next week. As it stands now," he smiled, "thanks to her, they'll be safely behind bars next week and for a lot of weeks – maybe years – to come."

"Imagine that," Mary sighed, shaking her head. "Our mother, a hero."

"Yeah," I said. "Go figure." Then, "Oh, oh, here she comes..."

Standing, Mr. Winfield made room for Mom on the bench and when he spoke, his words, once again, took our breath away.

"Anybody in there say anything to you about the... um... reward?" he asked Mom, just oh-so-casually.

"Reward?" Mom said, blinking. "Reward for what?"

"Oh... Just a little sum of money that's been accumulating over the months for the capture of those two scoundrels."

"Why... no," Mom said, shaking her head. "Nobody said a thing. You mean they were famous? Infamous? Really! Well I... I mean... What I did was nothing more than anybody would have done if they'd seen them, heard them. I certainly didn't do it for a reward..."

"How much is it for?" Mary and I howled in unison before Mom could say one more oh-so-modest, self-deprecating word.

"Oh... at last count, I believe it was around the two hundred thousand dollar mark. Give or take..." Mr. Winfield said, casual as all again, but covering his mouth to hide a smile.

I've always wished someone had been there to take our picture when he said that. If they had, that picture would've shown three faces, each with its mouth hanging open and its eyes bugging out of its head. He'd have had to be fast, though, that photographer, because it only took a second or two for the facts to register and then we were all talking at

211

once, laughing at once, and carrying on like a pack of crazed, out-of-our-minds, lunatics.

Mr. Winfield let us have our moment – a good, long one – before ushering us out of the stands. "I suggest some serious celebrating is called for," he said. "And I know just the place."

TWENTY

We celebrated all right! Long and late into the night while champagne corks popped and everyone out-talked every one else. It was like none of us wanted that special day to ever end. Well, think about it. What if we woke up next morning and found we'd dreamt the whole thing?

Next thing I knew, "We thought you'd never wake up," Mom was saying, bringing in a breakfast tray.

"I didn't know I had," I said groggily.

"Look at him," Mary said, coming in behind her. "You should have seen yourself dancing last night, Jeff. John Travolta, eat your heart out."

"You didn't look any too swift yourself," I said.

"Fight it out when I'm not here, please," Mom warned. "Today's our day to gloat."

We never left my room that day. Heck, I never even got out of my pajamas. It was neat. Like when you're sick and everyone comes in to make a fuss over you. Only it was better because I felt great. And all day we rehashed every single minute of the previous day, each one of us giving our own version of how we'd felt from when we'd gotten up that morning right through to the agony of that last race and what came after.

The weird thing about that was, when one or the other of us got going on what they'd been thinking or feeling at any particular time, you'd never have known we'd spent the day together in the same place at all, our stories came out so different.

And every so often we'd just sit in silence and stare at one another and shake our heads until one of us would whisper, "Two hundred thousand dollars," and start to laugh and we'd be off again.

"Think of it," Mary breathed. "Even after the IRS and the car for Steve you could have recarpeted that whole house if the Aldersons had gotten ugly, Mom."

"I know it," Mom chuckled and turning to me, said. "I called the Aldersons first thing this morning while you were still asleep. They said they'd heard about my "accident", from Clive – you know, Michael Angelo - but that he'd done a great job cleaning and touching up. And... you'll never guess why we couldn't find Al yesterday. It was because Clive got hold of him first thing and he was over at the house, too, replacing the damaged carpet and fixing the grout. Do you believe it? I can't get over those two guys giving up their Saturday to clean up a mess I made. And I was going to bribe them." She hung her head. "I'm ashamed of myself... But," she brightened, winked, "I'll give them both a huge bonus now that I'm... A-hem, a woman of means."

"See," Mary said. "I told you you were over-reacting. And to think of the grief you put us through Friday night and yesterday."

"I know," Mom said, looking shame-faced. "And I'm really sorry." She paused. "But think! If I hadn't dropped that can of stain, hadn't over-reacted, we'd never have gone to the track to find Al. Then what?"

We were quiet a long time after that, each of us trying, I guess, to figure the whole unbelievable chain of events that had unfolded since a can of stain hit the floor.

"It was believing in that clue I got, the name of that beautiful, beautiful Bold Man's Wife, that did it," Mom said. "If she hadn't been running, I never would have tried to figure out the connection and I wouldn't have seen her or heard those two creeps and..."

"Not now, Mom... please!" Mary said, holding up her hands. "It's just all too weird. Too deep. Too far out to even think about right now. We'll all have to figure it out, each in our own way, and compare notes in, say... a year. Let's just be happy that gorgeous horse is going to be OK." She turned to me. "David called earlier. He said the vets had been able to give her an antidote intravenously in time to save her from any permanent damage. She pulled some muscles, got hurt falling, but looks like she's going to race again."

I felt tears sting the back of my eyes hearing that. All morning long, ever since they woke me up, I'd been wanting to ask about that horse but been afraid to hear the answer. To divert them, I said, "Hey! Let's call Steve!"

"We can't," Mom said quickly. "It would spoil everything."

"But this is an event," I argued. "A major happening. Let's just call and tell him about yesterday. He doesn't have to know he's getting a car."

"No. If he knows about the money he's bound to expect something. And it would take his mind off his finals."

"Well, let's just call and say, Hi," I said.

"We're too psyched," Mary said. "We wouldn't sound normal."

"Right," Mom said. "And we wouldn't have anything to complain about. That would certainly throw him."

It really bugged me not calling him though. It seemed unthinkable. As if we'd celebrated Christmas or something without him. It made me think of the times they all talked about stuff that happened before I was born and I thought, Now he'll know how it feels. It won't matter how many times we tell him about it or how much we describe it, he'll never know how if felt to be there, or say he was there, and I know how aggravating that is. And yet, if it hadn't been for him, and that kid stealing his bike, none of it would have happened. Wild!

Later, when he heard the whole story, he said that explained why every time he'd called from around that time right up to graduation, he'd never gotten a sensible word out of any of us and if he hadn't been so preoccupied with exams, he'd have hitched a ride home to find out what in heck was going on.

Good thing he didn't. A lot of changes were going on around the place and if he'd come in on any of it, he'd have blown the whole surprise.

TWENTY ONE

It was still dark when our two cars pulled into the parking lot at the University of Florida.

Of course, there was "The Car", the bright red Beemer that had been hiding in our garage for nearly two weeks. "I guess we're going to have to go back to watching TV, nights, after tomorrow," Mary said the night before when she and I were giving it a last, loving polish.

We really were going to miss it being there when we got home every day. Even Mom, who likes to say she isn't into cars, got hooked on it. "It grows on you," she'd say, sitting on the tool box after dinner with a cup of coffee just to stare at it. "It really does."

Anyway, like I was saying, there we were in the parking lot, Mom and Mary in the Beemer and me and David Winfield in his Land Rover.

He'd invited us to stop and have breakfast at his farm on the way up and he'd followed us. "Hey, I've been in on this since the beginning," he'd said, "It's only fair I get to be in on the grand finale."

I'll tell you more about him in a minute but right then we were busy, "Setting the scene," as Mom put it, so the car would look just right, parked the way they park it in the ads. And that was pretty hard to do in the dark. Setting the scene was turning into a nightmare.

For one thing the auditorium where the ceremony was going to take place had about a zillion entrances and exits and how were we supposed to know which one the graduates would come streaming out of? And then Mom had to know east from west so when the sun came up it would catch the car just right.

Luckily, after Mary had driven the car around the parking lot about ten times and parked it at ten different angles and we were all getting mad at one another except David who just leaned against his car and chuckled, the sun started streaking the sky pink and gold, solving the east/west problem.

"This has gone on long enough, Mom. I think we should just park it way off to the side in some shade," Mary called, sick of the whole business and worrying about the damp taking the curl out of her hair. "By the time we all get back out here, it's going to be so hot he won't even be able to get in it."

"Shut up," I snarled. "Don't put any more ideas in her head. Just park the damn thing and let's get out of here."

She ignored me, so I said, "Let me out!" and she slammed on the brakes and I got out and went to stand beside David.

"We'll miss the whole point if we just stick it off to the side somewhere, Mary," Mom called, sounding impatient and stumbling because her heels were sinking, for maybe the tenth time, into the unpaved surface of the parking lot. "I'm ruining my heels," she'd moan softly each time she sank and then raise her voice and continue where she'd left off. "I thought we agreed we want it right out in the middle where he'll have to fall over it. I just don't see why you're making such a fuss. We went over it a dozen times at home. Why do you think we're here so early if not to park it in the one perfect spot? You know how I hate getting up early."

"OK, OK," Mary yelled. "In the middle. Well, it's in the damn middle."

"A little more to the left though, sweetie," Mom called. "Move it over two more spaces and back it in. That's the view I like best: three-quarters from the rear."

"Sh..." Mary began, starting the motor again.

"Ma-ry..." Mom called warningly, looking towards David.

"Women," I muttered, hoping he would know how much they were embarrassing me.

"They might not look it," he laughed. "But they're actually having a wonderful time."

"I hope you're happy Mom," Mary shrieked, braking violently and getting out of the car. "You've got the cops here now."

We turned and sure enough a squad car was bearing down on us, the revolving light on top of it turning each of our faces a cycadelic orange as it passed, its headlights picking out Mom, heels sinking in the dirt again and Mary standing furious, hands on hips, beside the BMW from which the stereo blared Jimmy Buffet as though he was there, live, in concert.

A couple of runners came puffing by and stopped to watch, panting and dripping sweat as the two cops, leaving their car motor running and headlights on, got out and walked towards us.

"Are you people having a problem?" one of them asked.

"Blew out my flip-flop..." Jimmy Buffet complained.

"Turn the radio down, Mary," Mom screamed, taking a step towards the officers and sinking again. She lunged and grabbed onto one of them for support.

"No, officers, none at all," she said, and then, "Oh, dear..." as in straightening, she dropped her purse, spilling its contents every which way.

"My mother," I groaned, hurrying forward to help. Everyone had the same idea, even the runners, and we scuffled around in the brightening day, picking up Mom's weird collection of junk while the officers looked on, stony-faced.

"Just setting the stage for a graduation gift, officers," Mom twittered. "Maybe you can help us. Which doors do the students come out of after the ceremony?"

"The main doors, ma'am."

"But... They all look like main doors to us. You see, this car is a graduation gift for my son and we want to park it just right."

"And they wonder the world's going to hell in a hand basket," the first cop muttered, turning away in disgust.

"You want to make a man out of your boy, ma'am, you oughta make him get out in the world earn his own car," the other cop said, walking slowly around the BMW but looking at Mary who ignored him.

"He earned 95% of his own education," Mom spat, all acid, "...completed a five year program in four. I'd say that's a pretty good work ethic for starters."

"Couple more hours and this lot's gonna be so full it won't make no never mind which way you park it, kid's not gonna see it," the second cop said, sounding friendlier. "I was you I'd park it off someplace quiet. You leave it here you risk getting a nick in it."

"Oh!" Mom gasped. "That would be terrible after all we've been through. But where?" she asked, her look pleading.

"How about the VIP parking?" David said, stepping forward so the cops saw him for the first time.

"Yes, sir!" the first cop said and I knew, right off, he recognized David and it blew my mind how everywhere we went, and we had been quite a few places with him since we met, people knew who he was.

What blew all of our minds even more, was how come we'd never seen or heard of him, before. "We just weren't moving in the right circles," Mom said. "How could we?"

"Face it," Mary said, "we weren't moving in any kind of circle. More like we were going around in circles. Getting nowhere fast."

"We were holding our own though, hanging in there," Mom said, indignantly, "Don't ever forget that."

Anyway, whatever it was, David and his name were working magic in our lives. Like when we went to the BMW dealer to buy the car and they couldn't get us a red one for four weeks and that one had to come out of Chicago. I mean, come on, Chicago?

"You'd think their job was not selling cars," Mom grumbled to David. David said not to worry and one week later a red one was in our garage. You just had to tell him what you needed and it was yours. Like the way he got us a table at the Country Club for the celebration lunch when Mom had been turned down by every restaurant in town who told her they'd been booked solid a year ahead of time. She'd never thought of the Country Club. Well, like, how could she? She didn't even know there was a country club.

"Weren't they booked a year ahead of time, too?" she asked him.

"Of course," he said, grinning.

"And you're a member, I suppose?"

"Of course," he said and we all laughed.

You had to laugh when you were around him. He made life so easy for us. Like the way you think life's going to be when you're a little kid and don't know any better.

"Look," he was saying to the officer now, "I'm sure nobody's going to object if I just leave my car parked right here and we put this little red job in the space reserved for me."

"No, sir, Mr. Winfield," the cop said. "That'll do just fine."

"You mean you were coming here today anyway?" Mom gasped, all taken aback.

"I didn't see any need to mention it," he said, laughing down at her.

"You mean you let us go through all this...?" she spluttered, waving her arms around the lot. Her heels started sinking again and she grabbed him to pull her out.

"It's your party, Kate," he chuckled. "I'm just here to help where I can."

So Mary got back in the car, turned the radio up full blast again and followed the cops to the VIP parking lot. In a way, it was worse there than it had been before because the cops had their own ideas about the best angle to show the car and the two runners had followed us and they gave their opinions and poor Mary got so disgusted shunting it around she got out and gave the keys to David.

He pulled it in just once and everyone agreed that it was the perfect angle and Mary burst into tears saying, "I already had it parked that way at least three times! It must be nice to be rich and famous!"

"Mary!" Mom gasped, shocked nearly speechless.

"What we all need is another breakfast," David said quickly, and putting his arm around Mary's shoulders, added, "Money's nice, sweetie, but trust me, there are a lot of things it can't buy. Ask your mother, she knows."

"I know," Mary said, looking shame-faced. "And I didn't mean it to come out like that."

"It's OK," David said. "Come on, everybody into my car."

At the restaurant we all ordered a bunch of stuff and when it was served, none of us could eat a thing. Not even me. Well, think about it. There was Steve just a mile away and he still didn't know *anything*. Only that we'd meet him after the ceremony. And there we were knowing that he owned the car of his wildest dreams, knowing every detail of "The Day", knowing that all our lives had changed and were changing so fast he was really going to have to hustle to catch up with it all.

And when he did - get the whole picture, I mean - I hoped he would help me with some of the questions going around in my head. Like, if we hadn't gone to the race track that particular day, would the car have come to us some other way? Would David Winfield have been wherever else that might have been? Would I have been able to get in if we had gone to the track another day? And what if Mom hadn't saved that thousand? What if? What if? I mean, it'd make you crazy if you let it, wouldn't it?

"And you think Steve will have answers to all that?" Mom gasped, when I told her about my confusion.

"Maybe. Just maybe. Maybe he believes in coincidence and luck and stuff like that."

"Honey, believe me," Mom said. "There really is no such thing as coincidence or any of those other things. If you think about it, you'll see that for yourself. Everything fit together too well. The timing was too perfect. Look..." she searched for words. "Our goal was to get a car for Steve. We thought about it, imagined it, and here it is. That's all. The hows and whys took care of themselves, just like I said they would. It really is that simple, you get what you think about."

Maybe she's right. About coincidence, I mean. Mary and I talked about it a lot and it just didn't seem possible that all the events, right down to the smallest detail, that led us to that day could have just happened by accident. It wasn't possible. Everything fit together too flawlessly for it all to have been "just" coincidence.

Another thing puzzling me around that time was how come all of a sudden I liked Mary when as far back as I could remember, I couldn't stand being near her. I mean, she was still the same Mary. Cussing. Putting everyone down. Exaggerating. Always complaining. Always whining. Still wearing her terrible nails and hogging the bathroom. But somehow, none of it bugged me anymore. It was just Mary being Mary, was all.

Listening to her talk with David when he came to the house, seeing her make him laugh, seeing she knew a lot more about different stuff than I ever gave her credit for, seeing her criticize herself, laugh at herself, as much as anyone else, I'd come to feel kind've proud of her.

Maybe then a lot of it was me? Always looking for her faults, expecting them, so that I never noticed her good points. And there are a lot more of those than I would have believed possible a few weeks ago. So all along, had I been proving Mom's point that you get what you think about? Did Mary act the way she did around me because that's what I always expected? Wuh...! Maybe Steve'd know the answer to that one, too.

Both Mary and I keep asking Mom if - more like, when - she and David are going to get married.

"I'm thinking about it," she says in a dreamy kind of way. "It's a big step though, not just for he and I, but for all of us. I don't want anything to come up after the fact that I should have thought about before. Right now I'm imagining every scenario, every detail."

"You don't need to," Mary said. "I've already imagined the whole thing for you. It's a done deal. I even picked out the dress I'm going to wear. Wait till you see it!"

"What are you waiting for?" I asked her once. "To see if Steve likes him?"

She'd been sitting at her desk in the den at the time and she swiveled around to look at me, her face going all amazed. "Why in the world would I do that?" she'd asked. And by the time she finished explaining, I wondered why I'd asked myself.

"Everybody," she told me, "is born to live their own life in their own way, not to please other people. This is true of David, too. We can't control others. That's what you're given a life for, to live it your way, make your own decisions. It's a responsibility. I can't live my life to please Steve or you or Mary any more than I would expect any of you to live your lives to please me. That would be terrible!"

"All right, Mom!"

"Not," she went on, "that I don't hope they like each other, because I do. Very much. In fact, I'd be very disappointed it they don't."

"I got it, Mom! All I wanted to know is what you're waiting for?"

"I just don't want to feel rushed, is all. For the first time in my life I have the time and the money to do things the way I want. I'm really enjoying that. And I want to get graduation out of the way and Steve launched. This place fixed up and sold... It's time to move on. "

"Where are we going to live then?"

"Where would you want to live?"

"Around horses."

"I don't blame you."

"So?"

"So imagine it. See yourself...."

"OK, OK," I said. "I know how it goes."

"What about me?" Mary asked. "Things're happening so fast around here nowadays I haven't had time to figure out what I want next."

"You've got the luxury now of looking at several options," Mom told her. "If you're ready for a place of your own I'll help you find it and furnish it for you. Don't forget I'm a whiz at decorating as well as a woman of means! Or you and Steve might want to..."

"Whoa!" Mary said. "Lord! I just don't know."

"No rush to know," Mom told her. "Take your time. Imagine yourself in all the various scenarios. The right one for you will soon surface. Then imagine yourself living it. It'll happen. Right down to the last detail."

So that's where we were that steaming May morning in Gainesville driving to the graduation ceremony. The closer we got, the worse the traffic. We wouldn't have had a prayer of parking if it hadn't been for one of the cops we'd met earlier spotting the Land Rover.

"Go on up the road a-piece," he called to David. "We kept you a place up there. My partner's looking out for you. We figured you wouldn't want to be too far from where you all parked that little red number."

"Very thoughtful of you," David called. "I appreciate it."

"I don't believe you," Mary sighed. "Everywhere we go people know you. It's unreal!"

"Mary, Mary," he laughed. "When you are as old as I am and have lived in just one place all your life, people know you."

"Here's another one that knows you," I said, seeing the second cop coming towards us.

"Right this way, Mr. Winfield," he called, pointing us towards a "No Parking" sign. As we drew abreast, he picked up the sign and we pulled into the slot.

"It almost doesn't seem right," Mom said, seeing the angry looks of other drivers still stuck in traffic.

"Don't knock it, Mom," Mary said. "It's here or walk for miles."

"I'm going to leave you here," David told us, "but I'll be in there watching for you and as soon as it's all over, I'll come back here to my car."

"But when are you going to meet Steve?" Mom asked.

"After you've given him the car. I'll be watching."

He started to walk away then, his tall figure striding through the crowds making their way into the giant auditorium.

"I don't like seeing him walk away all by himself like that," Mary said, watching him go. "It looks too lonely."

"You heard him," Mom said. "He'll be rejoining us right after the ceremony."

I couldn't help but hope that the "rejoining" would be a permanent situation from then on.

I must've fallen asleep the minute I hit the chair in the balcony of the auditorium. Well think about it! We'd been up since 3 a.m. The next thing I knew Mom was nudging me on one side and Mary on the other and I saw that the ground floor of the auditorium was a black sea of gowned students with more pouring in from all four corners and I felt like I was watching the ant farm I had back when I was about ten. We never were able to pick Steve out of all those hundreds of students and as far as I was concerned, the whole ceremony was a total drag. Just one long boring speech after another.

"Have you seen David?" I asked Mom when the kids started going up for their diplomas.

"What's that?" she said, dabbing at her eyes

"Have you seen David?" I asked Mary whose eyes were bone dry.

"You've been sitting looking at him ever since you got in here, dork," she said.

"I have?" I said. "Where?"

"Where else?" she said. "Sitting up there on the platform next to the Governor."

"Wouldn't you know..." I began.

"There goes Steve now," Mom interrupted us, hearing his name called over the loudspeaker. "Look, he's getting his diploma. Doesn't he look wonderful?"

"Just precious," Mary said, but she smiled at Mom.

"Look," I said. "He's walking right in front of David."

I looked at Mom and Mary and knew from the way they were shaking their heads in disbelief that they were thinking what I was and wondering how it could be that in this crowd of thousands, the two most important people in our lives didn't even know each other and yet there they were, not three feet apart.

TWENTY TWO

The outer sets of double doors of the auditorium had been propped open to let out the hurrying, excited graduates and their families and were letting in the stupefying heat of midday. We stood back of the shafts of sunlight that the doors had held back but still we could feel their heat while at our backs and above us, giant air conditioner vents blasted out their frigid air as though daring the heat to come any closer.

Most of the families had dispersed but still there were an annoying few who lingered outside chatting and calling to friends, the women dabbing at their sweating faces with limp tissues, the men loosening ties and unbuttoning the top buttons of their shirts.

"Don't they have any place to go?" Mary grumbled, peering at her reflection in the glass doors and fussing with her hair while Mom asked Steve question after assanine question, made comment after stupid comment, stalling, keeping us there until, with sideways looks, she could be sure that the crowds were gone and the cars parked to either side of the Beemer driven away. It had to be right. We'd agreed on that from the first. The car had to be the way we'd pictured it all those months. The way it looked in the ads. Alone. Aloof. Set apart from ordinary cars and ordinary people, waiting for the unsuspecting Steve.

From where I stood, a little apart from my family, I had watched the crowds churn across the parking lot and noticed that only the younger people gave the car more than the briefest glance. Like a brisk river parting and rejoining around a rock in it's path, they'd hurried on, conversing across its shining roof, nudging its sleek sides, even trailing absent-minded fingers across its hood then drawing away quickly, I was happy to see, as the sun-scorched metal fried their skin.

"What are we hanging around here for?" I heard Steve splutter for at least the tenth time interrupting Mom who was asking him if he'd remembered to get his roommate's address. "C'mon! Please! Let's go, Mom. I'm dying in this suit and gown. Didn't you say we were going some place for lunch? We can talk there."

"Take your gown off, honey, and let me see your suit," Mom said. "I never did see how the alterations turned out."

"Mom!" Steve exploded. "Later. Let's go."

"My program!" Mary suddenly exclaimed. "It must still be in there," and skirt ballooning, she whirled back into the auditorium.

"We've got a ton of programs between us," Steve yelled after her. "You can have all of them."

"No, that's OK," Mary called back a tad too brightly. "I want my own. It's for my scrapbook."

"Scrapbook!" Steve repeated. "The girl who hates family outings has started a scrapbook?"

"I'll come help you find it," I called after her, but she didn't hear me and Mom frowned me a No, so I stayed and took another quick look outside. I could see David sitting in his car. He'd taken off his jacket and tie and had all the doors open but he still looked like he was about to melt.

"What's she doing in there?" Steve fumed, watching for Mary to come back. "I bet you guys were the first here and if she doesn't get out fast we're going to be the last to leave. Don't you understand? I'm free! I'm through here. I get to do what I want now."

He stepped across the band of sunlight and looked out into the parking lot.

"Give me the keys to the car, Mom. I'll go bring it around so we can take right off. Where are you parked?"

"I don't know where they are," Mom muttered, fumbling through her purse. "Here, hold these," she handed Steve her sun glasses and camera the better to dig into the deepest recesses. "Oh, I know," she paused. "Mary drove us up. She'll have them in her purse. Why don't you see if you can find her."

"I don't believe any of you," Steve glowered, striding off into the auditorium yelling Mary's name.

Mom smirked as she slung her purse back on her shoulder and hurried to look out the door. The lot was empty at last.

"This is it!" she beamed at me.

I nodded and felt myself grinning like a jackass.

"I don't believe you two," Mom mimicked as Steve and Mary came hurrying towards us. "We're the last, the very last, to leave."

"Us and whoever owns that Beemer," Steve said, not seeing David parked off to the side. "That's the car I'm buying," he said, turning to Mom. "Give me a year and you'll see. It's awesome, don't you think? Exactly what I want. Same model, same color, same everything."

We were right up close to the car by then and he stooped to peer in the windows. "Come here, Jeff, take a look at the dash. Sharp, isn't it? And check out the upholstery. Leather..."

"I thought you were in a hurry to get out of here," Mary moaned. "It's just a crummy car."

"Hey, Steve," I called, the way we'd rehearsed so Mary could plant the envelope. "Come around this side and take a look at this. Somebody's put a ding in it."

"You're kidding?" he gasped, hurrying to join me. "Let's see." Anxiously his eyes searched the side. "You're crazy," he said, turning away. "There's not a scratch on it."

"Must have been the angle I was coming from," I said squinting my eyes. "Or the way the sun's hitting it. I could have sworn that was a ding."

"Are we going to eat lunch today, or what?" Mary sighed, backing away from the car and lifting her thick hair off the back of her neck.

"Hey, take a look at this!" I called to Steve. "There's mail or something tied to the windshield wiper. Jeez, with gold string even! Who'd do a dumb thing like that?"

"Must be an ad for something," Steve said, idly turning the envelope.

You'd have thought we'd all been turned to stone then, us staring at Steve, him staring down at his name in big black letters on the white envelope.

"It's got my name on it," he said, all confused.

"Be for real! Let me see that!" I said, louder than I needed to so the laughter choking my throat wouldn't get out. And while I checked out the envelope I kept my face turned away so he couldn't see the fool look I knew I was wearing.

"Hey, you're right! Mom! Mary! Come take a look at this. It does have his name on it!" I said, when I felt like I could control my voice again and thinking at the same time how easy it would be to hate Mom for putting Steve through this charade. I mean, why couldn't she have just given him the keys like anybody else?

"What?" Steve spluttered. "Who...?"

"That's your name all right, honey," Mom said, peering over his shoulder. "You're him. Maybe somebody knew you'd be coming this way and left you an important note. Some gorgeous girl with a party invitation, maybe? You better open it. In fact, please open it quickly so we can all get out of this awful heat."

I heard a lot of muffled noises coming from Mary about then and saw her face all red where it wasn't covered with Kleenex and darned if I could tell if she was laughing or crying.

"I don't get this," Steve was muttering as he fumbled the envelope off the wiper. "Nobody I know would leave me a note on some stranger's windshield. How would they know

I'd get it? It's border-line insane. Some jerk's idea of a joke, you think?"

"I told you college campuses are breeding grounds for morons," Mary began.

"Get over it," I growled, all of a sudden wanting to get the whole thing behind us. "Just open the darn thing so we can get out of here and get some lunch! Jeez!"

"Open it!" I yelled again, when he still hesitated, and he ripped the envelope open.

"It says," he began, and then his jaw was dropping and his next words were coming out in a kind of croak. "It says, 'Congratulations, Graduate! The car's yours! You imagined it! You drive it! We love you, Mom, Mary, Jeff."

Jaw sagging he looked from us to the car and back. "But... how could it be?" he floundered. "We don't... I mean, I know we can't afford... I don't get it..." And all the time he's talking he's running his eyes all over it. taking in every detail.

I saw David Winfield walking towards us then, his jacket slung over his shoulder, his grin as big as any of ours, and Mom and Mary were hurrying towards him dragging Steve between them, only Steve wasn't looking where he was going. He was looking back over his shoulder at the car. His car!

A big shiver ran right through me then out there in all that heat and I knew it didn't have anything to do with the temperature. It was because everything was just so darn right. Every dream we'd ever dreamed was happening right in front of my eyes and I wouldn't have wanted to be anyone else, anyplace else in the whole world. And in my head I could hear Mom's voice the day we went to test drive the BMW, asking,

"You want to dream little, Jeff, or big?" And I let out a whoop thinking, Man, as long as I live, I'm dreaming BIG!

The End

TUT® Adventurers' Club Oath

"In the face of adversity, uncertainty and conflicting sensory information, I hereby pledge to remain ever mindful of the magical, infinite, loving reality I live in. A reality that conspires tirelessly in my favor. I further recognize, that living within space and time, as a Creation amongst my Creations, is the ultimate Adventure, because thoughts become things, dreams come true, and all things remain forever possible. As a Being of Light, I hereby resolve to live, love and be happy, at all costs, no matter what, with reverence and kindness for All.
So be it!"

Take the Oath online, at <u>www.tut.com</u>, and begin receiving your FREE, personalized, daily, never-before-published, "Notes from the Universe" via email!

TOTALLY UNIQUE THOUGHTS®
...because thoughts become things!®

Launched in 1989 by 2 brothers and their cool mom, TUT® believes that everyone's special, that every life is meaningful, and that we're all here to learn that dreams really do come true.

We also believe that "thoughts become things®", and that imagination is the gift that can bring love, health, abundance and happiness into our lives.

Totally Unique Thoughts®
TUT® Enterprises, Inc.
Orlando, Florida
www.tut.com
USA

About the Author
Sheelagh Mawe was born in Hertfordshire, England.
Today she makes her home in Orlando, Florida.